CW01335766

You Can Accomplish Anything with a Good Pair of Shoes and Enough Tobacco

Epilogue to A Universe of Discourse

Max Dariush Baker

authorHOUSE®

AuthorHouse™ UK
1663 Liberty Drive
Bloomington, IN 47403 USA
www.authorhouse.co.uk
Phone: 0800 047 8203 (Domestic TFN)
+44 1908 723714 (International)

Published by AuthorHouse 09/19/2019

ISBN: 978-1-7283-9353-7 (sc)
ISBN: 978-1-7283-9352-0 (e)

Print information available on the last page.

BOOK 1

THE LABYRINTH AZIMUTH

THE END

Noesis lay back as Taqua made eddie sounds in the curling waters. A carp came flapping fleetingly to the surface, breaking the surface tension with its dorsal fin, imbibing the water skaters to scatter to a new area of disturbulance.

Noesis splashed Taqua with cogent coy and said,

"A carp. Prithee, what tails does it tell you?"

"It tells me, of all the things we've been through together. The thousands of years on Erith, the wars with the Spider race, our survival, of the secret we share, the beautiful secret. However, most of all, Noey, forgive me, it tells me of my love for you, but will I ever know, will I ever really know of the love you have for me. I will not leave you. You know that don't you?"

Noesis came to the surface a took a deep breath.

"Our secret belongs to us. I have seen you with your mates, proud of our accomplishments, but you know they'll never understand what we have. You open your mouth and the words spill out, but their ears do not hear. They are deaf to the screams because they cannot see the Love, our burning love, in that moment, that kept us together, and, Alive. Alive with survival, alive together, and the secret, life itself. So, you see, Taqua, we have thousands of years more together, perhaps, at this very lake, with our new adoptive family.

We both made it to K. You have plenty of time to understand that, time itself will show you, I will not leave either – except perhaps, to jaunt down to the Lake of Hubris and fetch us both a new batch of Golden Virginia.

All the while, Taqua, had rolled a new one, one handed, as he recalled Spartac's myth, in his left hand.

"Let us share this, and remember Spartac."

"To Spartac!" as they exchanged breaths of heated fruity air.

Then Noesis added: "The emotional historians, still, after all these Doses of time, cannot understand how he made it, ALONE!. May they never fully understand the secret we share."

"As cool as Miles Davis." Added Taqua. "That's what Spartac would've said."

And they said together under the deep blue blanket, dotted with the weaving of the stars:

"As cool as Miles Davis!"

Noesis tensed, leaning against her left elbow and sat up to join Taqua.

"Who would ever have guessed", she said, "That we could empathise with infinite agony and find God on the other side, for knowledge counts, and

God knows something about the poor spiders' pain, something, for the rest of our lives we'll not have to worry about again.

"We're running low. Got any Holborn?"

"Na, swapped with dust with Duke for menthol tips." She said.

"Looks like a trip to Hubris then, I'll go."

"Let's go together today." Privately proving to him that she would not leave either.

"Odd tip, that of Sparti, he sent to the Bull Frog. The lake of Hubris is our triumph and we adore to fumar, cancer cured so long ago its like an antiquated BCG. His nemesis, the thing he loved to do most most. Sit at a café, contemplate and smoke with a coffee, but even after the brow of the mountain of life, his fear of A.I., he just could not and would not quit this beautiful habit. The lake is for our children.

Then, Noesis and Taqua made love.

After, pulses at 120, 125, Noesis said:

"Einstein was right, how could he have predicted our paradoxical non...time travel when time was as nascent as a zygote. Zenda received Spartac's concept..."

"Don't you mean she kept her safe?"

"Yes, of course, forgive me." She uttered.

"He made it back with his father's courage, and they shared the concept, just like us....wonder what they're doing then?" Taqua replied.

A Universe of Discourse

The Accoutrements of a De ned Rational Argument

"I will not leave!"

He screamed into the heavens with such ferocity that even those that reigned in Hades trembled in fear. Momentarily there was the smell of incense. The olfactory truth of countless spoken words. Those words secreted in unknown places throughout time and space. These sanctuary to all little creatures, Bull Frogs in Chiang Mai, Cows in Dharamsala, Ants trekking their long journey through a rainforest temple. Max read the index: 'To be Read', but apparently his sister, EllaBella, Loved ants too, so, Bella was alright in his book. Zach had eleven days to run nine hundred kilometres, the souls of his feet afire with trench foot. The fucking head fucker religious police in Iran. Everyone hates you, including Persia. Do you have any idea how raw your penis gets after two hours of constant fucking. This is from me to you. Issue my Fuckwah…I fear nothing…for

God's will it might be for you to kill me. I warn you... release your mind from eternal sex for the iteration IBID. Think of the pain? If that's not enough, think of the once thriving Persian civilisation. You nearly killed my Uncle for wanting Persia to thrive again. The bazzars and a Love of children, just like Italian culture. If you try to normalise your crime IBID, you'll be hated forever. Allah's mercy, has limits. Be under no illusions, I Love you, for one reason, infinite faith has honour. Muhammad taught....faith, in faith, in faith, in faith, in faith, in faith....ad infinitum but Iraq inserted a word when you were not looking..... revenge. You made a dreadful mistake: kiss this 'To be read' a clear the mine field my son, I shall live to fight another day. Don't you think it should have been t'other way round eih? With Love from Max.

Zach saw the contrast of the good, that beautiful odour, graceful to the spirits, revealed adrenalin in its isolation. Anxiety washed over him as he felt the demonic presence. Too many he thought. But he suppressed the fear and focused on a future too distant to touch. The amplitude of his longing deepened. The waves of probability came crashing down with the second affirmation:

"I will never leave!"

He screamed again, bursting capillaries in his larynx – coughing up red mucus and then, laughing at the blood and the myriad demons who gathered, in his now contorted vision of unreality. Two hundred thousand.

Zach's mirth was a driven power of love, up till this point a love of adventure, of careening on blades, the bladed wheels, and also, the wheel of folded steel forged in this fire of azimuth. To coax a friend into happiness and say....

"Well mate – at least we will die together."

Zach wished not to endanger his friends, and the monsters knew this. They knew he was alone. They could sense thrice with utter meaning these words:

"I shall be alone – for I trust L.O.V.E. more than you will ever know."

Zach's knees were weakening. Caps quivering beneath his fragile skin. He lost his quiver whilst masturbating, forbidden for training, atop an oak. No more darts of borrowed wisdom.

He had a teacher once, but he never told him about this. How could he? How was it possible to explain to a student that one day they must find the strength from themselves? Deep within. Many friends he once had. But not now. Only but a memory. He could turn nowhere else for help, only the immediacy of his own courage and faith. He found the identity he owned, too many ugly words. The accumulation of a lifetime of experience emerging from beneath his mind as the occasional definition resting upon nothing but nothing. Yet Zach found the nothing as only a something. The bedrock of the ungraspable. With a past derived from the emerging present and a future yet to be understood - the monsters took hold of his isolation,

"We know your incertitude. Feel our freedom – we look at violence and the evidence suggests that we are strong, stronger than you – therefore we are demonic and you shall be one of us."

'Not fuckin' likely.' Zach thought to himself.

"We know we have no master. We know that we deceive one another and we know that you do not know that this is the only life."

"Ha!" Zach spake thus.

"We are hedonists working toward nothing. Nothing as nothing. Can you resist our secret: everything is as it is, nothing from whence we came, nothing from whence we will not go, and, we can manipulate all religions and philosophies with a simple thought: there is a basic contradiction for anything other than the nothing we worship. Give us your soul and we will show you the emptiness you seek. We can see your fear, so now, become one of us; and now that I see that we have you....do not underestimate the power of good."

Zach entered time to take time to think, a hidden life that would emerge in more fortuitous circumstances, later, in a hospitable conversation.

'I am outnumbered two hundred to one. These chthonic are far smarter than I imagined. How to beat these fools. I know….I will pretend to be servile. Act out the voice of a life without heart and return its words. So, he says to me not to underestimate the power of good. He thinks that I am already subjugate, so, I will entertain his confusion and, deceive. It is not my way to contrive intention, yet, Zeno of Elea, my old friend and mentor, please forgive me, will I ever see you again. I am so sorry that I am not strong enough to simply die at the hands of this bastard. I am so sorry….I wish to live. And so, the feign of servility and this stolen sentence, useful to me it is…and so….. very well….I will not underestimate the power of good. But I lose much in this exchange…..if I ever find my friends again they may never understand me… kneeling before a king in Hades! But, I never signed the paper they burn. Just, peeked at the small print. I caught sight of one word, 'conditioner'. But I did share their bottle. What the fuck was in that! I fear the worst. Perhaps there are liquid bottles of glass. Perhaps I should have known. Perhaps I am destined for the Hell I would so willing go if god is, and required for punishment for crime of drinking the unknown blood of the Golden Child. Ah! My soul already in danger, and this is why I fear a life without friendship.

Of course they will forgive me. So....Zach think, how do I recapture my love of friendship. Again, it is mine because there is hope, therefore I will hide it in the one place they will never find it. I will hide it in the trust of the human spirit. Now this is something I can believe. I can build my future with this. Existential love since Hesiod asked Zeus. But what can defeat the spirit of the gods, for they live in us all and it is ours to make the right choices. These fools that crouch before me....are they so ignorant as not to even brink on comprehension.....since the Upanishads, love is the eternal law. As concealed I must even from myself, I will kneel, and the love in the life of the human spirit will find me'.

Zach replied without a tear for his broken honour:

"I love you world....goodbye."

'My stolen truth, my stolen fearlessness. How will I survive without them. These do no work images, only empty words – even our great culture has no mandala – just a tepid remembrance – but I remember those days – images within a grain of sand.'

As Zach kneeled he licked his fingers and touched the sandy ground at his feet. Concealed in pitch night he felt the grains. Each one. Singular. Always. He saw his teacher and offered this poem to the air around him.

'Teacher. I remember you. So many voiceless sounds speaking to me of my young soundless voice. Schizoaffective disorder they all it. But my father speaks to me in an interlocution responsive in a material implication that is an evidence they cannot, and refuse to acknowledge. My spirit mutilated by their weapons of pure hatred. Quetiapine, an antipsychotic, refunes like TCP. Or root beer! Those words I struggle to recall, touch me to the depths of my soul even when I cannot find my soul. I would swim across the ocean for you, Ajahn, in a heartbeat. To Io and back. Nothing within the eons since the dawn of ostensive mathematic time can break the honour I know will one day reside between us once again, when I return home. God, my philosophy has broken me in half, I must find the courage to find that once this atheist cannot deny the propositions concatenated on the page. You are the collective voice of heaven, and heaven knows I should have known they were evil, because, of the paper they said they'd burn before me, their evidence in the fire. I should have known what could have been in that wine. I'll do anything....please.... forgive me.'

To remember what was spoken over candle-light, in the meandering chiaroscuro of deep consciousness. Zach recounted for himself a foothold in the axiom of human suffering. There are at least ten thousand people crying right now because they have lost someone close to them. That is about one cubic centimetre a second. One litre a day. About one ton a decade. And the village reservoir would be filled within the eons since the ostensive quantum cosmology cannot ascertain the exact dawn of mathematic time. We may, after all, still be living within the big bang and to reach enlightenment would be to find that two friends live in the real world. It is difficult to be the guardian of one's friend as one screams onto the battle field exclaiming 'death before dishonour', because there is no answer to war except the smallest prayer for the well-being of a little ant.

This, the sonorous gift to the world may reach the stars in their dawn of life and may often be so strong in its gentle solitude that it is the teacher of teachers. Revealing in a little rainbow of light that even though there is war, and war has no answer to war, friendship survives everything. To teach as this prayer one must trust that those that can be taught form a union with the search for peace, giving up the resting place of personal security for the prism of a raindrop made of crystal. To reach out to a friend and carry their burden. What if this burden is too much and one has promised a friend to carry it till the end of time?

Then out of nowhere Zeno replied – a vision of social truth, his society to come – the home he will find. In these words they wished to say,

'I, we, are principally here, for you, to convey our sincerest apologies of the issue that has beset the heart of your life – the heart that your feelings persist to wish to be a part of a tradition reaching back to the dawn of Hellenic culture. The burgeoning requite of the undenied name.

'Remember your vision – that far away conflict of inhumane animal- screams. To fight with steel – steel touches steel. To fight with your soul these things you risk to lose – your truth, your honour, your sanctity, your sacred friendship and your friends. We are proud of you – continue – you will win – you will find your future again. And together, united with your friends once more, life will be as it should be until the gates of heaven dream you into a life where you only say goodbye when it means happiness.

We give you this':

then Zach heard a mighty roar. A growl of a thunder-clap rolling across a mountain-scape. Zach could feel the isostatic fluctuation and with this voice of protection Zach spake thus to the demon, adopting the thunder growl of the mountains,

"Master ('tosser' Zach said under his breath) – I will never underestimate the power of good. Trust us now, I have signed with my heart, now burn this higher evil, and we will, all of us gathered here, in these woods at the noon of night, evinced with a spiritual power to make black the hearts of the powerful good. Follow me...I am Satan. Bet you didn't guess that this was a trial of your conviction! I will take you to the best of the good. When we meet, simple reverse psychology, tell them you hate them, tell them that hate is harmless, and if you find the courage, tell them your real name, so that they will be crippled with a poisoned heart and will be impotent to find the children you use. You will then be free to live in the hell that Shaitan promised, the hell you have fucking forgotten you beautiful person. Constant ejaculation forever in this life and the next."

Something unholy clouded his spirit as he kneeled but Zach still knew, somewhere, he was alive. He remembered the spark of enlightenment from an old friend. He remembered a priest in Christian priest in watford offering him and his friend, Zorn, shelter from the biting wind and the stinging rain. Zach's first introduction to a religion that could be trusted. And a man in his future dreams stepping out from where the walls hide shadows; from a nowhere embittered by the embrace of destruction - "I don't know who you are or where you come from but thank you." 'Thank you', Zach whispered to himself. Three memories of friendship. Enough to keep him going until he was alone once again. To open his eyes and coming to, he felt the worded wind once more and a figure upon yonder terrain, with such gait, only to be his son - Hyphen.

That night in the black red unlit light Zach cut all ties to his own history – his friends and spiritual masters – alone, solitude, deep amongst an unbroken darkness – waiting for a time to undermine the confidence of that which tries to deny life its own spirit of truth. The honesty between two gentle hands creating worlds through the frequency of touch and the much anticipated kiss. For this Zach would gladly die. Such paradox. Once the clapping hand, twice the begging hand, thrice to live and then, the fourth.....to sit. The soft touch of unspoken words, two collapsing electrochemical fields. The gaunt wait, for deceiving in death and death to deceive creates not a thing. So, alone, Zach touched one finger to another, self-life, self-love and all too immediate now was the philosophy of his own abiding existence. Responsible he was for his child and his son. Only if his friends found him, half beaten to death, cursing over the torrid morphemes and praying for his immortal soul would he recover and find his way out of the labyrinth azimuth.

Taqua explained to his son, when he was fifteen, just old enough to understanding where he was when he held onto the memory of Spartac, and of Spartac's collusion with Zach:

Imagine being brainwashed for several years that time in this life lasts forever. Now imagine that you are in the blistering dark, frozen, naked, crawling on broken glass, for mile after mile after mile. Also, convinced, that to stop meant the torture of your mother of the same fate. With a broken back.

With his improvised constructs, he would kill the ignorant demons, one by one, all of them, if necessary. Carefully assessing each to its own. Showing every quarter to forgiveness, every chance and beyond this, if they stepped over that line drawn in the sand, the line that even they know of. This line – we must not submit yet, only when this child wishes for complete surrender. And Zach, always searching out for those errors, those points in self reference that have no a priori. In Hades this was easy to figure out because it was his very own soul that crossed the line, his own line at that.

What they knew and what he knew they knew together. Zach valued life and at all costs would protect it – and so, the stolen wisdom of friendship would find its true home once they knew the strength of a small gift and maybe, just maybe, those hard to distinguish down here of genuine heart enjoying a pot of Mullah Light, would discover again that they were cherubs once and in their mutual enclosed environment of defined space they would wink at one another –

"I understand friend, this is scary business and we are together in the depths of Hades, walking to freedom amongst the few and the many that truly belong down here."

To wait for a time when these chthonic would lose their shore footing Zach considered that he would have to crawl for near eternity, for eternity within this life was all that they really knew and, sadly, all they really needed. He would wait and maintain compassion, a distant love for those caught within the throws of hatred. This would be easy, Zach thought, for compassion and time are two things that I do understand.

And so – the myriad – gradually flanking him – cutting off the spiritual supply lines to his mentors - of that which for what Zach wanted anyway – waiting for the third affirmation.

Zach reflected on his life as his Chi was immersed in single pointed terror. He was well aware that ever since Homer recounted the debt of the gods, so many angels had fallen on the battle-field before him. Success was by no means guaranteed. This was no quixotic quest – yet what choice did he really have. Once shown knowing. Once revealed suffering there was really no way to deny that which love knows - so, prostrate of Zeus and proud of Gaia he stood beholding those thousand foot unholy abominations breathing neutronium alloy.

"I shall not leave".

The thought to himself as he let his mind into knowledge of their blind eternity, 'I will emancipate those angels captive within the dreams of pain. And for the rest? Just as well really, that even proud eternity does not last forever.'

The eyes of Zach were released from their turpitude once he saw the way out of the labyrinth, having once made the commitment to leave when eternity was lived.

Hyphen – the son of Zach waved, approaching the cave enclave of Zach's vision of time chasing. Zach was unaware of both the fractal patterns of the retina and his son's approach. Hyphen was upon the brow of yonder hill. The parallel stream of change bringing the two closer within conventional space-time as well as a simple conversant nation betwixt father and son. Dedication, unbefuckinlievable dedication. There's a reason that word is underlined in word in red. Max's intention, that no other would suffer his fate, to live an unknown life of rectitude at a café somewhere. Now I can share this secret with the friends of D7. We'll fuckem, just like they fuckem. Respect! As my father said to me:

"Dad, I say fuck it, and get an unsurmountable task done,

You say Fuckem, because of the cruel hypocrisy of all but a few,

What shall I say to my child?"

"Fuckem all", He said. My father was God, perhaps only D7 would believe that.

Hyphen shared everything with his father – he toyed in his youth of twelve years of hypothesized lives past, of wishing himself an oriental wordsmith – of Gaia and affection for the ant and the bumble bee need no explanation for a life of simple service. For Hyphen loved words to such depth that he could taste the rosewater by any other name. This was the conventional wisdom of all ages and all retreats and he was humble enough at this tender age to wish for nothing more than conventional wisdom – not seeking the unknown name, so as to attach to his being for the psychosocial remembrance of a life once lived.

For this was Hyphen – this was how he thought. If this author, Zach, were to contrive a contemporary cavalcade of weary epithets – he was gentle to the degree of homophobic empathy. A magnitude of feeling. Allowing the life unknown to him to be the union of an asymmetrical dichotomy that his father sought to understand for the sake of the humble townsfolk.

Zach wished to run before time ran out – to find the concept to give to his son. The idea of life, to sit within the community and be at rest and perhaps asking for a little more – maybe even the community of a good woman.

Hyphen with knarred stick in hand right – father – allowing a little morns light to stroke his squinted iris – half opened his eyes and the to and fro of the ocular junction as one might notice looking out from a wagon in motion, watching the world rotate counterclockwise facing right and in the direction of travel. Eyes flicking with thought, strength and controlled penetrating fear. There was no turning back. He knew that insanity was a real possibility and would have to be dealt with when the time came.... this was a difficult acceptance, for there is rarely a reception gilded in material implication for an unknown spiritual life. Except that is where religion lives. For, for Zach, there was no religion of humanity, only the humanity of religion. At once departed, pessimistic and expressing cathartic empathy, and forgetting in the slumber of his left hemisphere:

religion lives, alive is the humane spirit and together we will find the unknown name.

Zach stared into the fading stars.

'For you, I do not know your names. I will name you Zarnath. Zarnath, remember a man once lived if I cannot find my way back, for it is my intention never to return, never, never. Only if the unknown journey has an end at the end of eternity can you return to me this message of the man I must find once more. Science, before I leave, I want to say.....we've been the best of mates for a long, long time and I am quite sure that you understand me even more than I understand myself. Look into my heart and you will find, I do not wish to be remembered because I fear the death of feeling.....I wish to be remembered so that I can return to my town with answers. Perhaps even the answer to war'.

"Hi dad."

"Hello son."

"Where you been the night?" Enquired Hyphen, fully cognizant of his father's dreaming life.

"No more the night – for yesterday evening is the same this morn's sun, and the morrow. And betwixt, the solar motion upon ordinary sleep and its own awakening to the world, awake, awake I was – shining in mind – illuminated was my world. You know. The usual escapades – fighting monsters.....tough night."

“You’re telling me – you never guess what Asal said yes afternoon. Spun me out man.”

“And what....was this....something about unfinished lists?”

“You could say that.....I simply asked her about the world I feel from her when she’s quiet. Sensing guilt for crying for the self, guilt for the tears of other people’s suffering and guilt because sometimes it feels good to cry. She just came out with a koan that’ll last me a lifetime.”

“Let’s hear it....”

“There is an exception to every law,
Except that is, for an exception to this.
Therefore: There is an exception to every law.”

“Thank you for sharing this little secret with me son.”

As Zeus strolled out of his slumber, sitting and smoking on the rings of Jupiter – a future already made – blowing the smoke into the sails of a solar ship he was mildly impressed by the way they parted. Zach gently shut his eyes and folded his arms as Hyphen at once stepped into the direction of the complex rainforest.

Zach and Hyphen thought together as they both parted. One in transit, the other in stasis.

"We are not alone."

Zach thought...

'How could I have been so ignorant – here is my friend, at once forgiving, there for me and understanding – who knows – maybe I am a good father after all. I somehow taught him to think for himself. And lo, what he does with freedom. Kindness. Understanding. And not even the word forgiveness for in me he sees nothing to forgive. Indeed I think that we are not alone – maybe I'll see him tomorrow. And I wonder what my beloved intensions for that little gem. I dare not intrude upon her teaching, but I must discover for the will of a world for my son, always there for him. Our home to his child.

We are not alone Zach cried, and cried. For the 'I' was within the koan of trust.

Quietly, masking the intensity of his feelings Zack spoke to the stream.

"World please – I can't take any more – these tears do not cease but the pain remains – tell me, in your infinite wisdom, what is the use of tears?"

Then the world replied within the sound of the trees, the leaves, the croaking frog and the whispering clouds:

'You cry because it is that you understand those distant without the tears that really belong to them. Let your salt with me and I will take it to the ocean. You will not notice the descent to the abyssal planes and the gradual dispersion of your grief. Think now, whilst you fight the battle with eternity. This sky, my mother, these trees, my companions, have watched you. We wonder why you reject your own freedom. Surely this is a losing combat. But you have made your journey and you see its end, so then do not seek the end but live in the evolving moment. We tell you what Zeno could not. I have seen many of society come and go and much iron has been left to these waters. Find the strength within the rocks at my ox bow. They will turn to dust, but not within your lifetime. Like the rock, try to accept your destiny. Give what you can slowly and do not fret that you lose yourself when you concentrate upon stepping your path for I will take care of you when we both form union with impermanence itself'.

Zach then began to step through his mind. The world he inhabited was new. So new he hardly recognized a single thing. Yes there were trees but what was a tree. Yes he had friends but what was their abiding continuity. Impermanence spoke of enlightenment but this was just an avenue. Zeno never told him about this. A new beginning where the past arrives without invitation into the moment and the future was to be built of his intention.

‘I shall not conceal my faith and will ask no-one to adopt beyond their own freedom. Some townsfolk thought me selfish but I know about time and what time can do. I will express my faith not when they are ready, and trust that they trust friendship between one another, greater than love for teacher. For time will take me from this world and often I wish it this way for this identifying pain is tremendous. I will lead them when they find the balance I seek, together, between friend and teacher. The ability to reject if teacher offers the question of love – to return his error – ‘no master – love is not a question – love is king, up here – high. Teach me not this and I will remember you friend yet leave your side.’

Thus spake Zach:

“The isolated antithesis of Bella is the confine of the unknown depths of our own fears. When the antipode of our hopes is a mere chimera of the entity we give life to through our faith, then, for the faithful there might be rest and forgiveness. For impermanence, the approaching form, defined only in spatial abstraction, if one wishes to know the eternal mind and forgo the knowledge of one’s own soul, then the fears of reflection are the anxiety of creating the life we inhabit with our conversation. Yet, beyond the ineffable state of such a perfect paradox, a state of which its unreality is unidirectional and only existent upon its own domain, truth is expressed simply because truth demands it. For the a priori singularity of the plurality of the Greeks and Dravidians of antiquity, each thought is a reflection, at its zenith, of such an identity achievement, of a divine eternity and one can sit at the limit of information and light, resting under the umbrella of the gods. A complete manifestation in that moment, a single thought stretching into a known infinity, connected to the companionship and humble embrace of the imagination. Such acceptance, found variously in individuality, is expressed in this world, preoccupied with the verification of mathematics, as the distant fracture of physical space. Fracture, the end of social dichotomy, the promise of omnipotence, and the anxious love that would tear us away from such a fragile world, for those who understand their own happiness would rather live in this possible world, in the past of their future, and defending the hermetic ideal of renunciation. To inhabit one's world, within the world, a faith in faith entails the love that crosses the boundaries of one thought to another, one defined feeling to the next, one self-reflective sentence to another sentient life, one decade of peace to a different future. And, so the purpose of truth is fully realized when wisdom protects the sacred heart of innocence and two people can find each other through the darkness and say 'you make a difference to my life'.

In this world the unknown form of potential personality emerges from the primordial soup, engages with its own creativity and finds the trust, beaten out of a tortured soul, the trust of one who gently touches the hand of another and in the creation of a new world both affirm the axiom that is so hard to believe. The necessity of plurality, built upon the structure of nothingness. Through the void we all endure a walk across an endless path, determined to find truth, find our soul, find the heavens or each other. Truth is not an empty word. It touches the incipient beginning and our hope for a future vanished of the suffering that knowing cannot extinguish. Truth and the courage to adhere to it, define often, our sense of desperate isolation and charges us with the will to walk forever. Where once we asked why, to find our parents, now we ask why, when our questions are exhausted. Why can it not be, on the cusp of why not? That plurality is not necessary.

The invisible teacher explains, like the sentient stream, you cannot know me twice, yet listen closely……I do not exist…..it is you that exists. And with that, Zach was detached from a Zeno that never was, and, set adrift in an explosion of space. Time and the many was many years away, a path as complex as a cup of tea. Five hundred and seventy two chemicals. Each, folding according to complex and fluid laws, some bound within Newtonian mechanics, some lost in the vast tendrils of differentiated statistics. The sweet water. Oxygen and commuting negative electrostatic forces somehow forming the defining characteristics of and with a shared couple of H's, of purposes so varied in nature and within the body, that filled libraries in a world, a world as yet unknown to Zach, that would take a god a lifetime to master.

ZACH S PARTICLE

Particle 3-gamma was small. I mean very, very small. It was his job to be small. That was what he did. He was the physical manifestation of the concept of the utterly minuscule. What he knew about the smallness of things was anyone's guess because he was also very quick. It was hard to catch what he was talking about. One could observe, obliquely, his effect though – for example: when a black hole got a bit big for their boots, so proud of their solipsistic accomplishments, he would coax the quantum dualistic creations to reflect time upon itself. This mirror would reflect all realities, including that of the non-existent, and the black-hole would have to look at itself in its own nothingness.

"Am I?" it would say.

And then 3-gamma would reply…"am i?"

3-gamma was the epitome of the paradox of self-identity. The harmlessness of a word or two that could make even infinity go…

"eih?"

And then, not realizing that it had asked a sort of question, infinity would go on about its business of keeping sentient life in order, but with something new. That something was the gift of the fool, for, the fool knows something knowing does not. The fool knows that happiness does not belong to systems of belief. So, 3-gamma imparted his gentle question, just living his life, and most importantly, saying "hi" if there was a "hi" out there to be heard. He didn't think his life extraordinary in any way, not even when sharing number with red giants or gamma bursts. Number was the particle/theory equivalent to a cup of tea. Red Giants could rip through an entire solar system, so magnificent was their strength that they were deeply feared, and yet 3-gamma abided with their company for a short while because he never stoked their pride, with a wit that was deeply yet casually concerned for the well being of their circumstances. 3-gamma saw that their honor and conflict was bound within social constructs that yearned for a teacher. Not 3-gamma being an instructor of the sort they sought, but compassion for their plight: compassion for the law they lived under, the law that fights in the name of defending something they are, within, too meek to feel they can understand. 3-gamma had begun life as the generation of a new concept in metaphysics. You could say that this was his past, but when you're this small time can do some strange things. Albeit to say, Zack thought him up when he reached the first stage of his enlightenment, space. A pervading continuity of form that penetrated every quarter of time, unmistakable as the bedrock of the many. Perhaps this was why 3-gamma understood the living paradox so well. Not just the noetic form of contained discontinuity, but the effervescent questions that could bring back to life a dying spirit. A spirit, like that of the red-giant, that had no power over his destructive destiny and seeking, in the corners of reified knowledge, sanctuary from what he could not hide from his own soul. On the third sip of number, 3-gamma explained in quantum imagination that he had to leave to attend to other concepts: something he would later regret dolefully, but left the giant with an explanation of reality:

"I go to have breakfast with my friends."

3-gamma hopped on his negative dimension illusion creator with optional leather interior and off he went, zooming between interstellar clouds, caught a wave of fluctuating space-time - a remnant of a long gone collision of two black holes and then eased up on the dark matter, calculating with ridiculous precision just the momentum to impress his mates as he would coast to a stop right outside the pub. Cloudy, as they called him, 3-gamma's best mate in the whole universe, had heard last century, well, in fact the last hemi-demi-semi-milli-anno-second, of a thing called a 'pub' that their creators used to use to 'get pissed' and 'have a laugh'. So, with the methodical harmonics of superstrings, gorgeous curvy superstrings, he constructed the 'pub'. The creation was primitive yet fascinating – a single valence shell that vibrated cheerfully so they called it 'too squiggly'. Too squiggly was circled in Hyphen's text book by the adept hand of a class mate, complete with the caricatured musings of their earlobeless physics teacher Mr Yates. Cloudy laughed out loud as Hyphen explained that Yates was also a trendy Wine bar. What the heck was 'trendy'.

"Let's all be 'trendy' and go into the 'pub'", said Cloudy almost under his breath and it was... 'funny'.

"What's 'funny'"? asked 3-gamma, then for some reason they broke down in 'hysterics'.

"Were not even in the 'pub", fingering inverted commas, 'and were already 'pissed'".

He said pissed in a new way, material language was intriguing. The confinement of matter somehow lent itself to absurdity. 3-gamma thought – heaven knows what we're gonna learn when we actually get through those valence shell doors.

By the time they were thoroughly bladdered they went to the bar to order their first pint.

"I'm sure something is backwards here", said 3-gamma.

His mates called him three. Those who called him three knew him best. Approaching the bar 3 suddenly realized that he recognized the neutron... just standing there, and 'just' was how best to describe neutron. He just did things and when asked that question that red giants worry about, why...he would just say...just, as if he were waiting for more words but seemed confident in his thoughtful solitude. 3 knew him way back, or at least neutron seemed to know him. Neutron was one of those particles the wise respect and leave well alone...a kind of knowing he possessed that one comes across in a handful of instances in a life-time, if you've got your eyes open. The kind of particle that is born with a foundational knowledge – understanding that seeking wisdom can be the folly of the spiritual materialist....better to let life be and accept any teacher of love - friend.

3 and neutron met briefly on a stony beach on the south coast of England. Neither Hyphen nor the child had been born yet, yet both felt the presence of 3, but as I said, when your as small as practically nothing, time can do some strange things – even cure a father's past of a lifetime of brutality. 3 gamma looked out onto the intersecting ocean and felt a question that was foreign to his analytic mind – the concept wasn't bound up with the morpheme but the magnitude of a searching question coming from a heart that needs answers to war. War had devastated the unknowing world in such ways that could not be quantified. The burden of a son to alleviate the grief of a father, grown

up in the bomb sites of London, searching for his own deceased father through unwritten books and unasked questions. What is the answer to suffering? Related, not on to the human condition but transposed onto the unthinkable. The unthinkable and the isolated antithesis that wore the mask of the real. Broken friendships that hadn't even the chance to casually meet eyes at a village café. The animal screams that Zach had heard in his transcendent empathy, a far away conflict with no honor, broken trust, broken, the trust of humanity that lies hidden in the depths of our social identity. The question 'why?' echoed for three thousand years from those many unheard places. Ripples of mistrust that philosophers, theologians, psychologists, struggled to uncover of true origin - in metaphysics, in faith and in the relative-probability of complex feeling relationships. So...Hyphen fell to his knees and hoped he could stop himself from screaming...Why!!!. Just when he was hoping beyond hope, in that twilight, that no-one would see him at his most vulnerable, Neutron approached from the distance. The two of them, knowing the question, knowing each other, their spirits together, briefly in a world that was unique to them. Neutron held out his hand and Hyphen calmed. It was safe, there was genuine friendship. It wasn't so much that they shook hands as shook their journey. As 3 felt this new word, imbibed with such feeling, Neutron said "just".

So there was Neutron and there was 3.

“Wanna pint?” Said Neutron.

3 was a little startled and then wondered if he should ask a good question whilst he had the chance, who knows when he’d see him again. A good question, significant and concise. He wanted to understand a friend so naturally he said… “why?”

Neutron pulled the pint and placed it on the counter, then he said in a tone that reflected a triumph and resolve over a long, long life… “Is this yours yet?” Then, uncharacteristically of the taciturn enigma of truth that 3 equated with questions designed for thought, Neutron waved his ‘hand’ ushering 3 to pull up a stool. Handed 3 the pint, advised him not to drink too much in his state of wonder and proceeded to explain the details of his knowledge for two hundred and forty thousand million years. Lucky for some.

By year two hundred and forty thousand million minus one (as 3 was too tired to work out the proper number), he was a bit tired. Exhausted. So he acknowledged, exhaustion, and swallowed the way home. Back to his maker, as neutron explained, back to where the subtleties of thought that was he, back into the arms of Zach to give him what Hyphen, his son - needed.

Zach’s knees were aching from sitting lotus all night. It gave him a good excuse to plan a different trajectory for his motivation, so, he got up. 3 remembered Cloudy and Zach laughed: ‘well I’ll be’… he said to himself.

Gentle Fire

As Zach stretched his back bone he felt the vertebrae click into place. He untied the knot in his pony tail and shook out his hair. Fresh morning. He knew what he now had to do. His future was to be made of thought relating to feeling, an unending journey fitting for the end of eternity, yet he wasn't concerned with perfect form any more. Infinite space had dissolved that illusion. His intention was now motivated by the unveiling of the true origin of his nightmares. Not monsters at midnight under a copious tree, but worse, an army of the dishonorable, far away, thieving trust from humanity, real in its horrendous normality, and for some, causing a surreality that sent artists insane.

For the next two years Zach contemplated a particular voice of his dreams. Above the confusion he felt the resonance of such kindness of someone in pain and confined. This pleading young sound that seemed to represent all that was being lost. A trusting heart that waited for her parents to come and rescue her...an innocence that never doubted their relationship. That which knew that she would be born. That which knew her life and that which held the secret to unwaking sleep. This could only be a child…Zach thought.

Hyphen expounded for Zach on a daily basis his further insights into the 'I' of the koan his mother had given him. If there was…as Hyphen explained…an exception to every law, then, one may as well accept what we are and what we have. I am and this is. Zach had opened up a channel to that child by confronting his demons, and now it was his choice to let go of fighting in the dark and to help that child with his eyes open.

He convened with the elders in the forest and told them he wished for their help in finding the child he found.

Yenna, Zach and Hyphen stayed behind to sit around the fire after the other elders retired to continue in their various mediations. Hyphen revealed himself at these times like no other. He would let himself be immersed in the sounds of concern and insight, just happy to be considered in friendship when nothing was demanded of him. The koan would subside as his intellect relaxed. Yenna knew this and used these times to let him just be a child…at least…to remember how to be a child in the creativity of his soul. Zach and Yenna discussed in leaping propositions how to go about helping the kid, then Yenna said:

"We will not have to go far, at least not to begin with. There are those that will come to us – I feel it."

“Who will come to us?” Zach was tentatively afraid that Yenna was speaking of the demons.

“There are some in great need, they need knowledge.”

“What knowledge?” Intoned Zach

Their words, and Hyphen’s comfort with those careful words, mingled with the quietly snapping flames. Yenna, deep and solid, provided some of his life to intensify and make more real their secrecy.

“There is something wrong with time.” Said Yenna

“I felt that too. I felt it years ago but thought little of it. What is the significance of their time?”

Then a lone snap jumped to illuminate Yenna’s robe and head. The pleats seemed to mirror the parchment of his gentle smile.

“Zach”, he said, “They control matter. Whilst we transform our thoughts and make them real, they transform matter and make it thought. I think that they are in trouble. There are a few among them, on their way. They want to learn how to undo what they have done. Their matter is turning against them. They collapse space.”

Zach was horrified to hear this. If his journey to his infinite space could unleash the worlds he had seen, heaven only knows what this would mean for the world they all lived in.

"How do they do it?" Zach asked. His voice quivered.

"They are no longer doing it. It is doing itself. Information is being carried away with their hypotheses. As soon as they know they no longer need to know. They are giving up and those that come to us are afraid of what they can see what is happening to them. The worst type of lost – giving up without knowing it."

Spartac s Journey to Find Zach s Concept of Isotropic Space

Spartac's mind was lucid with computers. For him they were alive. He felt more at ease when considering the fragments of program that gave his quantum computer its personality, than when trying to understand the conflicting desires of the human mind. His research position at London University in the year 3121 afforded him the opportunity to investigate the interaction between the imagination and quantum fluctuations. His quantum computer's circuitry transmitted information through light refracted off trillions of stabilized electron clusters within a synthetic diamond sphere. Waves bouncing off of matter come probability. The result was the generation of information that was in tune with the human imagination, the surreal journey of thinking with light. The fearful thing that Spartac was aware of as he interfaced with the quantum computer, was that his imagination was answered by the computer before he had a chance to calculate the trajectory of his own future. If man could not imagine, Spartac thought, if time itself was not exceeded by the ability of man to exceed himself, and the quantum computer confined him to answers that were universally material, then, we could never be unique in our own ability to respond to the human condition. Life would become the condition of programming. Spartac anticipated the future. He was also, once, a futurologist. Quantum computers could draw energy from synthetic black holes and create matter, and, that matter would manifest itself amongst the living as an environment that would glibly be at their mercy. But the truth was worse, we would disappear from time, forgotten by time. The entire universe becoming concept and its limits as accessible as a walk down the road. Without these restrictions all creativity would be pushed to the margins of the unnecessary.

Zenda stood in the doorway of Spartac's little office. The archway of the entrance to the office was an undulating curvature. A fiber optic panel weaved around the office displaying the mood of his computer. Zenda's hips were the kind that held a young child effortlessly. She leaned, deliberately; piquing Spartac's interest, then, satisfied that men didn't understand women she asked him if he had the numbers.

"Do you have the latest report on the seven hundred and seventeenth level of imagination?" She asked.

"I'm still working on the fifteenth." Spartac replied.

"We need the seventeenth by Tue. The subject I told you about last week can't manage the uncertainty of communication with Alpha prime."

Alpha prime was a constellation way beyond the scope of Hubble III. Since 2068 quantum imagination was communicating with life far beyond the beyond. Philosophers had worked out that mankind had already got there. They were living in our future and could only return once we knew how to interface with their space. The down shot was, we could only interface with their space once we knew their quantum number, of which we could not know until there was direct communication. And so, quantum computers worked tirelessly with human imagination to calculate the exact quantum coordinates of their return. If they didn't succeed in this communication, Alpha prime could not return, could not set up the means of their departure, could never leave for Alpha prime and mankind would be captive within the photon-system - assigned to rot away as the diamond spheres created matter and slowly nibbled away at the human condition.

Spartac had a different idea. He was already working on the thirty seventh level. He listened as Zenda tick tacked down the corridor. Then he heard a short step and a 'tack', followed by a quicker pace as she returned to his office.

"Just one more thing Spartac," she said,

"These aren't your toys you know. You may be the best interfacer in the northern hemisphere but we have a job to do, an important job. You can't just expect everything to fall into place while you mess around creating consciousness."

"I assure you Zenda, I know what's important."

Before the institute Spartac was a futurologist working for a government agency. Nothing much had changed...mankind still seemed to need these quaint organizations. He and his colleagues searched through the most obscure philosophies of every corner of the globe. They all agreed. The human condition was in jeopardy of being lost in perception come form come matter. He was asked to leave the agency for proposing that the ability for questioning creativity be given to the public domain. There must be someone out there who held the metaphysical concepts needed. All the parameters the futurologists came up with pointed to infinite space. This was a moment of genius between them. Making the leap from conclusion to supposition.

At the agency two entire blocks were devoted to mind travel. During mind travel the universe is rotated locally and forces the physical form into space. The tragedy was, when the subjects returned their thoughts had been turned to matter and they had not the metaphysical concepts necessary to piece back together their own minds. In short, they went mad, bobbing back and forth between the real and the surreal. The last subject, of which Zenda was talking, needed, for the immediate moment, the seventeenth level of imagination, or so they guessed.

Within the hour Spartac had neatly bundled the seventeenth level and sent it to Zenda. For all the good it would do, Spartac thought. Give it another day or two and there would be another emergency, but he was too afraid to voice his opinions. The agency wasn't short on volunteers. Psychologists and philosophers who were overly confident in their appraisal of the real. Good intentioned beings who were let into the secret knowledge that either they find themselves in the cosmos or the spheres would destroy them all. Spartac went one step further…where would love go once the condition of life was lost. Would love start all over again as the entire multi-verse was made into protean life, begin primordial, searching for its beginning, searching for its purpose and searching for compassion. Those who were acquainted with destruction just saw it as the next stage in evolution, but for Spartac, evolution was just as flawed as mathematics when it came to searching for the origin of the searching soul. He was alone in his thoughts. He attended, again, now he had a brief respite between subjects, to his quantum computer to try and calculate the whereabouts of the concept of infinite space. But what Spartac didn't know, was that space was just the beginning. If and when the coordinates of mankind's return could be ascertained, there was more to learn, much more.

As to general relativity, the subjects within a rotating universe traveled for a linear eternity, give or take a bit of curvy space-time, and, they eventually arrived back in the present. The problem being that, everything was now an unknown, so, they could not ascertain within their own minds as to whether they had indeed returned. Relativity gave the means of conceptualizing the journey and probability mechanics enabled those at the agency to travel coincident with the sphere of the lone photon that was their universe, and return, in theory. The subjects knew the unknown, knew the coordinates but could not communicate what they knew. If mankind was to return they must not only communicate via binary probability but learn how to learn. They must learn that this was once the origin of the departure from their companions. Once there was successful communication the information gap would be closed and mankind would be free to travel for the first time to the places they had already been for trillions of years. Complicated stuff. So, Spartac searched for the concept of infinite space whilst Zach searched for the child.

Spartac excused himself from work after a brief altercation with head office. He went to the park to consider the implications of his understanding and intention. He could be struck off and worse. People walked by unaware of the fracturing space around them. Now and then someone would wind up on the other side of town with no recollection of how they got there. The press was printing more and more of these incidents, putting it down to some kind of biological anomaly, amnesia? The heads at the agency felt helpless, watching the world disintegrate, piece by piece. Spartac had to tell them what he had to do. He risked everything but he was so involved in government routine that he couldn't go it alone. He approached head office. He knocked on the knocking pad. That was head office's little joke, harking back to the time when there were doors.

"Enter!" Was a robust voice. The reverberation and rasp of its various levels - telling of the many commands of life and death decisions.

Quathe was standing by a model of a black hole generator and staring out of the window. But before Spartac could open his mouth Quathe did,

"I know why you're here. Zenda's taken a look at your calculations. Whatever you're up to tell me now. It looks as if you're scanning the world for the concept. You know what that means. The competition will be aware of our presence. You are aware of that aren't you, or, do you think you are smart enough to avoid detection. We've set limits for a reason Spartac. If they infiltrate our system they could sabotage our world and we might find ourselves on Mars!"

"Quathe I know how serious this is but we simply don't have the means to obtain infinite space. We are using matter. We need to use mind. There must be someone out there who knows. Just knows."

Then Quathe lowered his head and his eyes looked down and to the left, staring voidly at the black hole, and gave in a little as if he were regretting a wasted life.

"I know, I know. The agency hospital is filled with thinkers. Don't you think I see what we're doing. Very well. I don't know where else to turn. If you think you're that good – do what you must."

"If I succeed I'll bring them back."

"For heavens sake don't mess up. It's best you work alone, you'll be harder to locate that way."

"What about Zenda?"

"What about her?"

"Either she's with me," Said Spartac, "Or you get her off my back."

"It's best you work alone – I'll send her to B-block. I'll tell her you're needed for binary construction. What do you need.?"

"Access to a multi-frame quantum computer and an emotional interface."

In the instant of his response to Quathe's question, Spartac had already left the multi-frame behind. A small misdirection directed at the agency. He couldn't resist. As well as the search for infinite space he wanted to see the world. Spartac considered that the best motive for finding the concept, was adventure and exploration, since, these were central to his human condition.

Spartac acted instantly. To detach from the agency he needed speed. They needed not the time he had not, so in order should no-one track his progress and to truly be free, he moved. Moved casually down the hall, controlling his cornea to avoid emotional recognition from the standard corridor pace monitors. Entered his office and sat at his desk. Feeling the pull of his racing heart he packed all he would need into a small bag. The address book with concealed emotion chip and his false fingerprints and the updated version 9 retinal obfuscators. In his rush he did forget one thing though. Credit. He hadn't needed the use of the antiquated means of payment for years so naturally it slipped his mind. He could get as far as Basque on his ID, beyond this he hadn't thought. But hey, this was adventure – to discover life, himself and the key. Discovery, the key to his condition and within itself the key to the unknown. He glided down the corridor, heading to the Bank street entrance – so alive, in his mind he had left behind everything. Now, in this moment, he had no job, no home, and of course – no credit. If he left the borders questions would be asked by the agency, recriminations and in the worst case – returning back to London, with nothing to his name, and, a severe reprimand for revealing the location to the opposition. In short, he'd be up the creek without the ancient proverbial.

This was a one way ticket alright, but the stub had no destination. He made it to Callais, he considered in his subdued, frenetic worry, that the agency would know something was up by now. Yes, sure enough the electromagnetic frequency would have changed to reveal a suspected exit. Now he was entering the territory of frequencies little known to the crystal chip embedded in his little book. He consulted the chip through the false prints, that doubled as a synthetic hormone information transducers. Basically, it told him – be careful.

Within seven months Spartac had conversed with quadruple agents, hints of places of safety and potential sabotage – so he would prefer the occasional discarded half eaten sandwich and slept in ditches by the side of the road. He got used to the homeless life after a while – he got the occasional kick and a 'get a job you bum' but, hey, his life was more than that – and he was - he was out to find the concept. He found the first sign on the 15th May 14. A child, simply asked for some water without fear. Spartac gave the water without fear. Poor kid. So he let the harmony of that gift with his crystal chip and hopefully, when the concept was found he could also find that kid. Sadly, in this vast world, unlikely – evidence suggested that many angels died on the way to nirvana, but what more could Spartac do than to give that kid some water. The concept was far away in the future somewhere – the holy wo-man! taught that one should have compassion even in the face of the most terrible violence. Please look after that kid – Spartac thought. 'Holy mother – Zach thought – the mother loving concept! Love, gift from that beautiful child - concept here, we, come.' Thanks kid – I'll pray for you, thought Spartac.

Then the reality of the dirt street was illuminated with such cadence:

He watched as a new age guru meandered on by tapping a drum and singing so happy that she just couldn't care less that others were laughing at him, as they went out on a Saturday night, rotated their mind frequencies, copulated in the toilets, got pregnant too young and batted their brains until winding up in a psychiatric ward at 45. Well, some of them anyway, at least, my friend James.

And, as Sacred vagabonds,
Sell their wares on dirty streets,
He watched with fixing watch in hand,
The yogic woman,
And her dress of pleats.

Spartac, Zach as he now called himself, or, whatever you want to call him, found work with a watch-smith, tapping out 2.7mm discs of platinum – and in return had the safety of the local gangster's domain. At least he wouldn't get beaten senseless every other day whilst he worked hard.

After ten days one of the gangsters, Emile, approached him and asked him a direct question.

"How long are you staying?" probably wanted to know if Spartac was interested in regular visits from the local prostitutes, discount and all. Debt – servility. Of course, Zach wasn't stupid – a little intimidated that he nearly told him his real name. Not so stupid indeed – so, he called him 'friend' and talked to his heart – and his.

Heart

Heart, shine like that compelling sun. Please beat louder so that I can hear you above the whirlpool voices. Beat with the ferocity to match and surpass this drug induced psychosis; so that I can feel you beneath the insensate sternum. Beat so that I may know assuredly that some part of me understands that I am an honest man. And in this tenuous knowing I will ask 'what are you?' and you will say unto me 'beat after beat'. And then, seeking the gratitude of an unpaid laborer and within my foolish world of self absorbed philosophies I will ask, 'where are you' and you will reply 'beat after beat after beat.' If I should define you perhaps I will lose you. Is that your way of being free?

He found the child.

One particular day the heavens opened up, and rain like drops of thunder splattered mud high into the air. The tension rose and destroyed the emotion chip interface in his little book. Ho hum – life ain't so bad with nowhere to return. Hours later after Zach wondered how much water can possibly exist in the sky he lay back in a patch of tall, tall, grass by the intersection, wondering with his peculiar pattern of thought whether the grass would prickle his neck as he lay back and when the grass bent near the root, it did. This was a time of recuperation. He could not quite believe that he had made it so far. He was given his mission parameters three years ago to the day and he fought his way into a labyrinth of espionage and counter espionage so deep that in the end he worked only for himself. Aligning himself to the confines of his task was proving to be a mortal threat and so he blurred the edges, until, so far from home there was only one person he could trust, himself. He had to let go of his dream of returning home and instead built a new one here in Architravia, the intention of his mind. Those with whom he had reluctantly but necessarily become acquainted were his enemies, the enemies of friendship and reason, to their face he called them friend, which broke him, but, they were anything but. But was the word – you would not believe what they did with buts. The cigarettes I mean. I won't go into the details of the third word, for Zach was too scared even to visualize what he knew they did to Zach's spiritual friends. So Zach seethed with indignation as he was forced into the circumstances of the war of his humanity, to be cordial in their company – yet, Zach could also be rather smart - as he deviously implanted his hacking viruses into their cerebral mainframe, as he in turn became a part of their lives and he had to leave his behind. There are so many things that they can't prepare you for in training. His took four years. He was constantly having to learn and to adapt to their strategies. His most potent weapon was his anonymity and low rank. No one would suspect that he would have the clearance to apply the viruses. The viruses acted to undermine confidence, one of the most high level areas of social structure organization. He withheld his knowledge and learned within six months that they built their power upon behavioral categorization and if he enacted a particular category he could turn their own devices against themselves and they would have no means to grasp his intention, since, they did not have the category of security clearance to form such an offensive.

Perhaps I'm racing ahead, like the thoughts of Zach, we'll return to him in a little moment, like this hospitable conversation. Hospital – that's where 'I' am. But lets return to Zach. You might have guessed that Zach is somewhere new, yet, he had to conceal his identity from himself to protect his heart from the thieves. They might see the fragility of his vulnerability within his eyes and take advantage of him. The doctors told me I had a cute little bunny rabbit depressive state. I suggested that it also had an optional leather interior? Through art we engage with something so real, this story makes sense to me. I hope you are enjoying it. Anyhows – I don't really know where Zach is either, yet, what I do know is that he's gonna make it. I'm gonna make it.

'I'm gonna make it', thought Zach

"I've found the child, he's coming, and, I'll wait. By the way, heaven, if you're listening, "Let this little ant be safe."

Zach and the Hidden Journey

Zach sensed the approach of conflict as their harbor traded simple goods. For the last two decades their harbor had been open to the odd traveler that found their way, somehow through the meandering straights to their little part of the world. And little it was, for Zach's people saw little need to occupy their exploits with chasing matter. Instead they searched within and, lucky or unlucky, however you like to put it, those few like Zach were offered the chance of transcendental time chasing. This was a meditative technique employing sexual energy to reveal the destination before one is aware of how to get there. To make love under the copious tree, with his friendly-girl, both illuminating their communion with compassion for the world. Not, throwing away the orgasm into the past, but remembering their future together.

The travelers, curious creatures, brought with them such confusion so clear to their eyes. They seemed to be aware of unanswerable suffering. They called it torture. There was one who arrived mysteriously out of the fog one year, as the tales tell. It transpired that he was tortured so severely that he forgot his name. He mentioned nervously of a force without intention. A force so blind that it was its own master. Their part of the world had been largely forgotten after the Hyperonic war that, in the wake of the EM neutrino detonators, cut them off from most forms of modern transportation. Zach and his people, respecting the courage of his taking to water, took him, and few, to their mountain cupola. There to see the congregation of guru's who tried in vain for month after month to explain that the answer to what they called torture was to be found within. Deep within where the absence of a concept of existence delineates it own reality. Nihilism come freedom, and then to return. For most it was like teaching a brick how to float, but the nameless man's eyes began to sparkle that day.

Zach was dreaming in the twilight of his mind, still by the warmed rocks of the fire, of the nameless man with sparkling eyes, but none made the connection – that he carried within his sternum the secret of the name of emptiness, that only love can find. The man stuttered a few undecipherable words and his mind was so obscure not even Yenna suspected that this was the one who had found the child, the simple love that could connect two worlds and save countless others.

Zach was about to rise, and pondered briefly before lifting his heavy lids that he'd fallen asleep without realizing it, yep, still by the fire, quiet embers now, then, when he felt the ground beneath him pad, a quirky voice intoned,

“Enjoy your sleep?”

“Son, man. Cheeky of you sending me to sleep like that, I’d so much to get on with.”

“Well, you seemed to need it. Plonker, what on earth do you think you were doing these past few days? I must tell you now – you weren’t alone yesterday evening.”

“You saw that?”

“Damn right I saw it. Foolish man, those visions were so powerful I think even Zarnath could see them.”

“How the heck much do you know? Well I know, that, within the matrix, I know enough.”

“Sorry mate, didn’t mean to scare you or others.”

“You didn’t scare me, but the loneliness. I wept for you. You shouldn’t break your heart like that”

His eyes concentrated like a school teacher wondering how on earth the hapless student knew that. He turned and then approaching from where his son vanished, a messenger.

"The forest elders need commune with you immediately."

The messenger, Zorn, was beside himself with grief.

The elder turned to face Seshan with such reflex alacrity that he nearly jumped out of his skin.

"Leave now!!!, now damn it! and don't look back!"

Zach disappeared into his subconscious and wasn't to return for ten years. Yep, I'm doing OK too. Doctors told me good things about myself today. Think I'm getting better, I think.

Zach seized the command and then forgot where he had just come from. Such is not looking back.

He felt, somewhere detached, a plane of knowing where entities of illusion pass by and whisper, the silent echoes of an absent history embedded within Zach's sweat and heartache.

'I am here, no longer I am, you are where, feel me, and as a man, despair.'

As he thought, he once again attempted to hold his composure and live the presence of impatience, as he'd been taught. It was not working, not this time. This time was different. He could feel his subconscious welling up and insight would follow. Maybe it would be now. He followed the patterns of energy and intuited that it would be soon – where a chapter in his life was ending – maybe even beginning. He sat cross legged, hands cradling one another, and as he place great concentration lightly touching the tips of his thumbs together he gradually stumbled about his mental space trying to quench the thirst of his intellect.

It was not right that one man should delude himself into thinking that to find love changes even the stars – yet this was his life. Some time long ago the tradition of the woods captured the spirit of the material man – eons ago, and still living was the belief of his world that a single good thought can change even the passage of the stars. So, he held onto his traditions in the face of emptiness, leaned forward and with his momentum tensed and stretched his legs, leaping into the air and shouting once more.

"I will not.. ....leave!"

But when he shouted the firmament looked down with disdain. It peered down upon this lonely man. A man and his family and yet, as so many like him – unable to find security in companionship because the material world, or, the lack of it, no longer sustained the asymmetry and reciprocity of identification.

I see you, you see yourself, you see me, I see that you see me and we are now together.

As matter fell away, he saw that there was seeing, and finding no sanctuary in the endless opinions of being, and no logic in the matter-man states of intuition, he found his own way. I will not leave; and rather sentimentally explained to himself: I will die in battle.

The crushing paradox that would drive a man to such a conclusion was such:

If I am matter, all is equal and,
I must be, because I must.

If I am not matter, then all that was,
Is, and is endless and I am forever lost

The stars peered down upon this ludicrous summation of family life, on the brow of a hill, alone, with the company of logic and imagination. They did wonder who he was.

ZARNATH REACHED DOWN

Photons from epsilon prime never made it all the way to Zach's retina. Instead they unpacked their rucksacks at squiggly particle 4-delta, and pitched up their tent. The retina could wait, after all, they had been trekking for a thousand light years and were feeling a bit grubby. Photon lepto was on a covert mission to determine Heno's prime candidacy for star transformation upon his death. But, to be honest, lepto just wanted a holiday from the beta quadrant. All those stars were just getting too much, with all their,

"Ooh look how big I am."

And when you're a photon overhearing star conversations one can get a bit touchy. Lepto's traveling companion was a recently promoted quark called meso. Of course, he had no idea about lepto's agenda, he was a good navigator. Straight lines were his forte. And for his expertise he got a free lift. That night meso stayed up till the wee hours plotting a straight line to rod 168-B,

He thought that they'd better start black and white and move onto colour when they got over straight lag. Huddled under his sleeping bag lepto cracked open his rendezvous instructions, to meet quarks John and Tabatha in imaginary number word improvisation in 3 days time.

You see, as things get smaller, other things get bigger. Smaller and faster, bigger and slower unless you're a black hole in which case you're small and slow and no-one likes a clever clogs. Lepto was charged with interfacing with Zach's imagination and becoming one of the characters and influencing that someone's destiny, and that destiny was to be intertwined with the lives of the stars themselves.

The stars wondered who he was and had done for some time, year after year upon that same hill. He was so tiny and yet so full of the capacity to dent the possibility that freedom could not be found.

They tried to reach down to him with their morning light, a colour combined with the watery cold due, to form a hue that is a word that only the morning knows. They tried to tell him softly,

"We are the stars and you are just a man."

Letting go of the will to move the stars, Zach turned over in his mind, like a machine, walking through death with the knowing of life on the other side; the words:

"Life: where are you?"

With a gently childlike hope, the belief still persisting into his advancing years that the stars could be embraced in the cold clammy clasp of his cupped hands.

The stars mused. Could he not see that his arm was too short to touch them. Again, futile tears ceaselessly queued up and he clenched his eyes shut, seeing dark red patterns, the kind that cannot be drawn. Zach and 3-gamma caught a glimpse of lepto and meso's tent as they slept humorously, but of course Zach was not to know of their significance as he followed the particle around, always out of focus and just out of sight.

No, he thought once more. Why am I stricken with a complex that denies me natural humanity and will only call me to the nature of love itself. Why this pointless charade. It will mean one thing only. Either I succeed, find freedom and this pain never was, or, that there is such a seeming reality of which I am completely unaware that does not deny the past but literally is and yet somehow and impossibly divorced from the self.

I cannot keep reeling up in such a pitiful defenseless composure. It is strange that when I cry the world is right, something to do with tears, the release. The real sadness is when you know that you are alone and then you wonder about all the other people who are crying alone.

"I see that you see me!"

Unaware of the spirit of definition, 3-gamma sat whilst the trees and the empyrean angels saw. And often they saw too much.

The elders in the wood had ceased giving him overt instruction several months earlier. He was one of the few in the community who visited the holy men in the wood. He and his son Hyphen. They gave no reason, they simply would not speak to him. They would not climb down. Zach thumbed over every conversation, every gesture to find a reason, a purpose for their behavior and ultimately, his own life. This was a step, he concluded, only he could take. So, he chose his own path.

"I will never leave. Even if it is impossible, I will succeed," trembling over the will.

As he went deeper into his continuous state of mind he found himself becoming less and less frivolous in his attack on spontaneity. His friends all found a change in him. They did not like it but they tolerated it. He could not tell them the real reason why his eyes were so often swollen and blood shot. He felt, in a position that he thought was better suited to a forest dweller than to a sane country man. He could not tell his friends that he cried, indeed, why he cried for they were unaware of the source of their own condition – which travels the same ground under every blue sky.

First, there are those like Zach that declare an unborn entity and that this entity is unknown, unhappy in seclusion and should be known. And then the other. Those in the many who somehow find an enclave of happiness in the mess that is existence and commit to declare that such a notion of freedom is for the lazy and the ignorant. Well, I'm trembling again, in ward seven. I must be afraid of something. Paradoxes everywhere.

Now the colour of dawn was here. The stars were faded apart from a few stragglers.

Is it too much for a man to dream, does he not look foolish if his dreams are too heavy with the weight of un-accomplishment. What would life be without those who dream. He simply wanted to tell his children that the world was a safe place.

He did try to be strong and slowly prepare them for the world, and the life they were likely to experience was so peppered of misery. Maybe, hopefully, he thought, they will be stronger than I, and they'll find their place with the world and not simply in it.

"I will not leave."

He said again softly with a croaking voice. There I go again – probably afraid of the world beyond this psychiatric sanctuary – at least the psychiatrists seem to care – they care that I'm distorted and look way past the fact that I can't stop sh-sh-shaking.

He knew not much of the world beyond his own and yet he saw the whole world in the township. Some part of him longed for a home, way beyond his town, beyond any place, where even light could not go. To dive deep under water, through a labyrinth of black caves, and then in the silence take the isolations back with him into his town, to the city.

He thought about the potters, many pots.

He thought about fields, many fields.

He thought about the market, thousands upon thousands.

And then he thought about their homes: isolation.

Matter tells only tells you when you need it,
When you have it, it lets you forget.

It's hard to keep track of all the names. I'm at present, scribbling all these notes down on scraps of paper. Like this'll ever get published. And here we have, at his very own book signing....gibbering mehess. But hey, gotta hope for something, can't just expect life to get better all by itself. Gotto av sompetin to old on ta. Zach – the I'll never leave dude. Asal, beloved wife of Zach, Koan dudess. Spartac – futurologist with an interest in adventure dude. Hyphen – oriental wordsmith, son of Spartac dude. And Particle 3 gamma – him I like best, also, dude. Hyphen, meso, lepto etc. To be honest I can't keep up with the intertwining destinies of psychosocial identity.

There's some kind of permanence to be found in this plot – maybe that's why I'm enjoying writing this, helps me forget about the fire and make some sense of my life. I'll try to honor your time and bring some coherence to the intertwininess – maybe I'll find myself, maybe not but at least I'll give it damn good try. No, I'm gonna stop there – I can't bring myself to think about it. Long story short – this is the past, this story was published in the future of that past and now things are looking up. I'll get back to you in a couple of years; perhaps by then Spartac will have remembered his name and that Yenna might discover the child in Spartac's heart.

7 DAYS, 6 MONTHS AND 2 YEARS ON

To deal in the commodity of hope, eventually, I have found, the demise of one's teacher, be it one's parents, peers or life – holding onto the perpetrator of despair as the last bastion of knowledge – sitting in the electrifying seat of the mind, the severity of the sceptic of war. To be, to have lived the question to the max.

Yes, sometimes I stand alone, as all, yet the serpentine departure of discovery informs the sensitive proclivity, occasionally I do not need you. Stagnant stoicism perhaps or maybe intolerance. To regard friendship in similar respect to the question that has no answer – create something and step onto it, into and across the void.

The stepping stone I give to myself, and to the receptacle of your sight is something good, methinks. As I look upon the word: the word the child knew and the fool dances around, for as long as I breath and for as long as this journey has no end I will think of her. As she once lay her head upon the pillow, and her mother sang her lullaby, together in words, but now they are parted and she asks for water from strangers, these words heal my heart and perhaps they find their way in the world of reality as well; to pray.

So, I am presently pondering and wondering about those beautiful highlands. Armadale, a little town on the northern tip of Escoses. My friends will be arriving shortly, so, I'll fare thee well – with this sunset:

And beyond, yonder, where the beginning of meaning at this setting event, makes room for the twinkling of the wonders, that crown our sleep with a soothing sense of permanence, that is the young sanctuary of a child's drifting thoughts, to the gentle hand that strokes eyebrows with sounds of kindness.

Note to the register of sight: Designing a foothold in the axioms of my disparate experience, hopefully conveyed amongst interwoven destinies that we all find are not as simple as a conclusion, the conclusion this thus:

L.O.V.E.

This novel is not necessarily to be read as the destiny of the page. To be read as the following of words and the meaning that you may find within them, beneath them, of them, or a simple smile, of which, for me, as an author, would find most pleasing of all.

If you get lost, remember, someone gave a bottle of water to child in Dheli.

Prelude to Life

A name I had,
The letters of which,
Went lost in sadness.

There was death,
For a long while,
Solitary darkness.

Now I live and know it,
What can be there to give,
Not my name.

Each our is close to me,
When is dying,
When dying is time

Universes of Discourse
The Breach of the Argument

BOOK 2

THE CONTRAST OF THE GOOD

"I will not leave!"

Max screamed into the heavens with such ferocity that even those reigning in Hades trembled in fear, momentarily, there was the smell of intense incense in tents. The olfactory truth of countless spoken words. Those words secreted in unknowable places throughout places and time. Sitting Bull....said my teacher as I slammed my hand on the floor with such ferocity that the bone splintered like Tito Puente. He said...calm, these sanctuary to all little creatures, Bull frogs in Chiang Mai, any one of the cows in Dharamsala, India, bullet-ants star trekking their epic journey through our rain forest temple. After my teacher brushed a bullet and off my knee, he said: "Be careful the life of a bullet ant can be intolerable."

"Do you mean it's in pain."

"Stop playing games, you know exactly what I mean." "Te juegas con fuego." Said the interpreter and she ambled by. "Okay, I won't play games, I'll simply tell you. I'm playing with fire because Mai Chi Pit has rabies. It is my intention to investigate this pain and find her in the next life with a cure. The Dalai Lama says… 'Intention is everything'".

My Ajahn, then demanded a response. The kind of look you get from your Dad if you're seventeen and she's late, "Do you want to fly away." I knew precisely what he was thinking. 'Am I ready for Nibbana.' My heart yelled.

"I'm not leaving these poor fuckers behind. What about that man I saw on TV in the Big Apple. He'd just been released from the state pen for possession. No, home, rent, for a convict. Such courage. He said, If the world doesn't want me then at least I've got my guitar. How the hell does he afford flat wounds."

Max saw the contrast of the good, that beautiful odour, graceful to the spirits, revealed adrenalin in it's isolation. Anxiety washed over him as he felt the demonic presence. Secretly, out of psychic probing from his teacher at the roof of the Tripitaka library, where none of us farang, foreigners, seemed to go, he was alone to summon up a good fight. Little was he aware, that years later, he would meet the fight's master opposite the British Library in a little library when he was collecting images for an artist for a hospital display. 'Too many', he thought. But he suppressed the fear and focused on a future too distant to touch. The amplitude of his longing deepened. The waves of probability came crashing down with the second affirmation, this affirmation as arrived over a laddered fence at the Chiang Mai forest when he was alone. Something tip toeing his shoulder. Freezing! A tarantula perhaps? Waiting two long minutes. No, must've been a vine.

"I will never leave!"

He screamed again, bursting capillaries in his larynx – coughing up red mucus and then, laughing at the glops of blood and the myriad demonic that now gathered before him, in his now contorted vision of unreality. Two hundred and forty thousand million. Not to put too fine a point on it. Max's mirth was a driven power of love. Up till this point a Love of adventure, of careening on blades, the bladed wheels, and also, the wheel of folded steel forged in the fires of azimuth. To coax a friend into happiness and say…

"Well mate – at least we will die together."

Max wished not to endanger his friends, and the demons knew this. They knew he was alone. They could sense thrice with utter meaning these words:

"I shall be alone – for I trust L.O.V.E. more than you will ever know."

They knew he was alone, for he conjured the demons wrenching their evil away from the poor bastards smoking down to the butt.

Max's knees were going week, before the demon's master, of which the master is the non-deceiver in deceit. Quivering under his fragile skin. He had an Ajahn once in skin contact as he gave him the razors so that Max could feel just like a monkoniorum, however, he never told him about this. How could he? How was it possible to explain to a catechumen that one day he would be utterly alone and that he must find the strength from deep within. For that was the Buddhist path, to travel beyond, as Max discovered, way fucking beyond where there is no beyond. A butterfly of friends he once had. Proximity with friendship was not now. Only but a memory. Max could turn nowhere else for help, only the immediacy of his own courage and faith. He found the identity he owned, ugly words that the demons had held up a dirty mirror.

The accumulation of a lifetime of experience emerging from beneath his mind as the resting upon nothing but nothing. "I think' was the subject of his proposition', I think, and 'I am' was the predicate. Therefore, the copula was: therefore. Yet what he was being tortured and no longer allowed to for a copula, for that was precisely what torture did, denying the very basic need to form a question. When the copula became absent in Max's brain, the subjects and the predicate dreamed a life where copulation could not find any proposition with the predicate W.U.B.

The accumulation of a lifetime of experience emerging from beneath the seat of his noetic as the occasional definition resting upon nothing but nothing, bedrock of the ungraspable. With a past derived from the emerging moment and a constructed future yet to be understood – the monsters took hold of his isolation.

We know your incertitude.

Feel our freedom.

We look upon the products of our violence and the evidence suggests.

We are strong, certainly stronger than you.

Therefore, we claim copulation and you shall be one of us.

'Not fucking likely'. Max thought to himself.

'We know we have no master. We know that we deceive one-another and we know our master is actually, my friend, you! For when you suffer an absent soul, your crimes against humanity will be our king. We also know, our friend, that this is the only life.'

"Ha!" Max thus Spake, as **Lau Tzu** and poor old Nietzshe at the foot of Mighty Thor got together and found the copula where it was not, the one place the Demons would never look.

"We are hedonists working toward nothing. Nothing as nothing. Give us your soul and we will show you the emptiness you seek. We can see your fear, so now, become one of us; and now that I see that we have you. Do not underesti-mate the power of good!"

Max entered time to take time to think, think about 'being'. A hidden life that would emerge in more fortuitous circumstances, in a more hospitable conversation.

'I am outnumbered two hundred and forty thousand million to one. These chthonic are far more intelligent than I could have imagined. How to beat these fools. I know…I will pretend to be servile.

Act out the voice of a life without heart, run and hide, and return to one's enough its words! So, he says to me not to underestimate the power of good. He thinks that I am already subjugate, so, I will entertain its confusion and, deceive. It is not my way to contrive intention, yet, Zeno of Elea, my old Chinoise compadre, friend, mentor and god of, 'which effing pocket are my smoking accoutrements', cheeky sod, he's been playing that game for a million years and it still makes he and Thor chuckle. Please forgive me, will I ever see you again. I am so sorry that I am not strong enough to suffer his knife. I am so sorry…I wish to live. And so, the feign of servility and this stolen sentence, useful to me it is…and so…so true…I will not underestimate the power of good. However, I lose much in this exchange, If I ever find Té again he may never understand me….kneeling, before a king in Hades! Ah! That smarts, within this modus ponens, "If There are those, and of those – obtain the predicate - not understanding then is the a priori foundation is a soul in danger", 'and this is why I fear a life without friendship. Of course, they will forgive me. So…Max think, how do I recapture my Love of friendship? Again, it is mine because, within, is the a priori foundation of hope. Therefore I will hide it in the one place they will never bother to look I'm sure. I will hide my Love in the one place they will never find it. I will hide it in the trust of the human spirit. Now this is something I can believe in. I can build my future with this. Existential Love since Hesiod asked Zeus. However, what can defeat the spirit of the Gods, for they Live within us all and it is ours to make the right choices. These fools that crouch before me...are they so ignorant as not to even brink on comprehension...since the Upanishads, Love is the eternal law. As concealed I must even from myself, I will kneel, and the Love in the Life of the humane spirit will find me.'

Max replied to the king, knowing exactly how to convince it, without a tear for his broken honour:

"I Love you world....goodbye."

'My stolen truth, my stolen fearlessness. How will I survive without them. These do not work on images, only empty words – even our great culture has no Mandala – just a tepid remembrance – but I remember those days – images within a grain of sand.'

Angels at the Mill View

Max picked up one of the ample ends of Ganges' pile next to him by our bench. I called him Ganges because he reminded me of the Holy man from Rajastan.

"Ganges", I said, as he put the chemistry he showed me back in his pocket... "Why is Queen Elizabeth the Second so B.E.A.utiful?" Then I said...

"It's the numbers isn't it. That's why you're here".

He then took a small pad out of his inside pocket and drew me the descending curve of a catalytic reaction. Over the course of four weeks in the sanctuary he taught me much of that which I missed at Glasgow Uni, Environmental Bio Geo Chemistry. He never did tell me about the numbers. Must have been tough. Crawely. Creepy crawly spiders.

Pitch Night

As Max kneeled he licked his fingers and touched the sandy bank at his feet. Concealed in pitch night he felt the grains. Each one. Singular. Always. He visioned Ajahn and offered this poem to the air around him.

'Ajahn.

I remember you, just,

So many voiceless sounds,

speaking to me,

of my young soundless voice.

These words I struggle to recall,

Touch me to the depths of my soul,

Even when I cannot find my soul.

I would swim across the Pacific,

For you,

In a heartbeat.

Across the continuum,

If necessary,

To Jupiter's bolt-lightening moon, Io.' u

Nothing within the eons since the dawn of mathematic time can break the honour I know will one day reside between us once again, when I return to the home of our journey.

To member that which was spoken over **candle light**, in the meandering chiaroscuro of deep consciousness. Max recounted for himself a foothold in the axiom of human suffering. There are at least ten thousand people crying at this very moment for the loss of a father, the loss of a mother, the loss of a sister, the loss of a brother and the loss of a friend. This is about one cubic inch a second. One gallon a day. About one imperial tonne a month, and the village reservoir would be filled within the year, since ostensive quantum cosmology (a reworking of quantum states to the macro level of string theory) cannot ascertain the precise moment at the dawn of time. Ganges explained that, conceptually, Sir Hawkins was correct, that there is nothing south of the south pole. But Ganges believed his calculations correct, that, the event horizon of the observable universe was a continual process of renewal as the first singularity, the wake of the big bang, was a process of perpetual creation. We may, after all, still be living within the big bang and to reach enlightenment would be to find that two friends Love in the real world.

It can be difficult to be the to be the guardian of one's best friend as one Screams As Storm,

'Death before dishonour', because war has no answer to war, something that just needs doing, except the answer of a smallest prayer for the well-being of a little ant...

This asseveration of truth, the sonorous gift to the world may reach the stars in their dawn of Life and may be so strong in its gentle solitude that it is the teacher of teachers. Revealing in a little rainbow of light that to teach as this prayer one must form union with the search for peace, joy and happiness, giving up the resting place of personal security for the prism of a raindrop made of crystal, God's snow flake. To reach out to a friend in their hour of need and make the solemn promise to carry it until the end of time. What is this burden feels too great? Then the intention becomes time itself. The time of experience abiding in a continuum of what it is to be human, in dissimilitude from empirical time, yet both forms conjoined in the happenstance that the two forms of numeric structure, first the infinite infinitely-divided, second the infinite divided to a limit of 2, are structurally identical. For the second structure, the empirical a priori of quantum mechanics, the first number is two......One what?

Then, out of nowhere Zeno replied – a vision of social truth, his society to come – the home he will find. In these words they wished to say,

The Call of The Gods

'I, we, are principally here, for you, to convey our sincerest apologies of the issue that has beset the heart of your life – the heart that your feelings persist to wish to be a part of a tradition reaching back to the dawn of Hellenic culture. The burgeoning requite of the undenied name.'

Zeno, with his bloody head fuck paradoxes, just for a laugh in a private joke. I can see it now, Achilles sparking up after he finally caught up with the tortoise. DJem the Tortoise. I'll tell you about him later. He's in a deep quiet depression because he taught me about China. They had to dam the mighty Yangtse, he said, but they let the side down. They're a symbol to the world, as cheesy as it may sound, of being at one with nature. Jem's Tai Chi master smokes like a trooper and when he looked into my eyes with Qi like a gaseous giant, I knew then, I ain't gonna die too soon. All I could do was to say, thank you☺

Remember your vision – that far away conflict of animal screams. To fight with steel – steel touches steel. To fight with your soul these things you risk to lose – your truth, your honour, your sanctity, your sacred friendship and your friends. We are proud of you – continue – you will win – you will find your future again. And, together, united with Jawal once more, Life will be as it should be until the gates of heaven dream you into a life when you only say goodbye when it means happiness. We give you this:

Then Max heard a mighty roar. A growl of a thunder-clap rolling across a mountain-scape. Max could feel the isostatic fluctuation and with this voice of protection spake thus to the Demon, adopting the thunder growl of the mountains,

"Master ('tosser' he said under his breath) – I will never underestimate the power of GOOD!"

Something unholy clouded his spirit as he kneeled but Zach still knew, somewhere, he was alive. He remembered the spark of enlightenment from an old friend. He remembered a Christian priest in Watford offering **he** and his friend, Zorn, shelter, fire and blankets from the castigating howl and the freezing needle point rain. And a man in his future dreams stepping out from where the walls hide shadows; from a nowhere embittered by the embrace of destruction. – "I don't know who you are or where you come from but thank you." THANK YOU, Zach whispered to himself, and pondered, perhaps the Eastern Block. Three memories of catalytic friendship, jump starting a fusion reactor in his heart. This was more than enough to sustain him until he could be alone, by himself, once more – probably sleeping behind a bush somewhere in Kilburn. That was the place of my father's young heady teddy boy days. He told me how he burnt the vivid uncensored photographs from Auschvitz brought back by the GI's, he just couldn't stand the pain. But knowledge is knowledge and it was a pain we shared together our lives long. Not such a pretty Buena Vista day, 'train comes and I know its destination, it's a one-way ticket to a madman situation.'

To open his eyes and coming to, going with the confidence of a sleep-walker, he felt the worded wind once more and a figure upon yonder terrain, with such stance, only to be his son – Hyphen.

That night in the black-red unlit light Zach cut all ties to his own history – his friends and spiritual masters – alone, solitude, deep amongst an unbroken darkness – waiting for an opportunity to undermine the confidence of that which tries to deny Life its own spirit of truth. The honesty between two gentle hands creating worlds through the frequency of touch and the much anticipated...kiss. For this Zach would gladly die. Such paradox. Once the clapping hand, twice the begging hand, thrice to Live and then, the fourth perfection.... to sit. Piercing his mind like a sabre tooth insight, he saw the holy man from Rajastan. Dredds down to his feet. Finger nails inches long, smoke yellow and curled - evil in wisdom. Emaciated beyond recognition. He was drinking lambs blood from a human scull and then he said in his transcendent empathy.

'I do this to understand the pain. You're not the only two survivors who understands Auschvitz.'

Then a crow swooped over head, Cacow, Cacow it crawed.

The holy man spoke with a Hue Stench of burning flesh:

'I exist within the collective memory of the planet as various archetypes and deities. Search for your Love, the Love of your Life, the soft touch of unspoken words, two collapsing electrochemical fields.

But, beware, the gaunt wait, for deceiving in death and death to deceive creates not a thing.'

So, alone, Zach touched one finger to another, all he had at this moment was self-life, self-I-Love and all too immediate now was the philosophy of his own abiding existence. Responsible he was for his child and his son.

In the months prior to the choice of the ignorant path, when Max was about to lose his name and become the facsimile of himself, Zach, he left thousands of messages with voyeurs that happened, all to be named Claire. Remember. This is a one-way ticket, and I have no remuneration left in my stolen soul. I shall need the trust of humanity, the view of a windmill, my name's not Dan, I won't be let back into normality if his friends found him half beaten to death, cursing over the torrid morphemes and praying for his indestructible soul. A picture of lunacy, like waco, of cults, and bolt action snipers. They might just see, a glimmer, of something inside the crazy wisdom of the short path, that peppered the rare liver that Lecter was a fight. For the foolish farang, racing around to attain a short lived power, it was only called the higher vehicle because, observed, it may take only twenty years, yet on the inside a mind of perfect lunacy, that desires a permanent end to the fire in the mind, and holding onto a single hope: that the word compassion might mean something, or even worse, that the word Love would cripple a dark and aged soul. “Is it worth it?” A good student may ask. ‘This depends on two things, you not kill, and you do not kill yourself, does the short path seem so short to you now?’ If only all the sun’s could shine together and beckon a dark sky with its history painted on the retinue of ordinary kindnesses would he find his way out of the Labyrinth Azimuth.

Zach was consumed by the unconsuming fire, with his improvised paradiddle and bo-didly systems of time change jazz, he became a monster. Had the king won or was this just a hint of an ongoing discussion, to make a deal, and it was a tremendous life, killing the ignorant demons with a lexicon of untraceable spirituality, tying up everything in sight and then also destroying the memory of a broken Buddhist law. Intention is everything: do not Kill. He vowed to himself, as he ripped Buddha’s book apart, I will kill the demons, one by one, all of them, if necessary> The master of his master said “If I stand in your way, strike me down.” Well Buddha, I will pay for this crime against Life’s law, evil intention is mine…but, fuck you, in this moment I adore being evil, intention, find answers to war, find the correct sentences to liberate the mind of a child...for the conversation continues...I can break this law for those I kill are dislocated from my time and space. It would be like being charged with a murder of the killer of one's own father ten thousand lifetimes forward in time from this one being lived. Yet still, the intention is there. To defend innocence.

Class, in 1945 the war ended. Yeah right! To be Schutzstaffel you only need to be as old as my wonderful physics teacher, Mr Yates. And the final solution: a colloid without a meniscus. Heaven and hell become one, no trace after an apocalypse of a heart strong enough to remember this beautiful planet, and, then, the classic psychosis....no one will be around to judge this evil deed if I murder this person that represents to me all that I hate...hating everything.

So, as Ajahn grudgingly accepted the responsibility for this gifted yet reckless student he let him into the Higher vehicle, the Tibetan way.

Max sat. Teacher sat. Ants sat, and even the wind sat, and he said:

"To wait for a time when these chthonic lose their shore footing you will need to wait for a near eternity, for eternity within this life is all they really know and sadly, all they really need."

"Who? Asked max quizzically.

"No more games, you know who."

"Oh, them."

"Wait and maintain compassion, a distant L.O.V.E. for those caught within the throws of hatred. For it is, along the short path it can be difficult to make out the difference between those who have had their mind raped, from the rapists. Remember, I know more about you than you realise. When you wake up!" As Ajahn clicked his fingers.

Max was asudden within the bright environment of his mind.

Oh, hi Ajahn.

Ajahn said: "Remember and feel no shame, for you are truly good. Thank you for the many Baht but you will need this to get to New York. I have spoken with the highest authority and you have a flight chartered on Saturday the fourteenth and twenty five minutes to seven, PM, until then, use this Baht to explore our civilisation."

"Why will you not accept my gift?"

"Wai exactly. You know what a wai is yes…..as the teacher put one palm to another and nodded his head. Try our custom with the ordinary people of Thailand, and I think you may begin to smile again. We are, after all, the land of the smile. Until the fourteenth the gods have bestowed mild weather with a beautiful tab of sunshine. Please accept this gift." As Ajahn gave the empty envelope back to Max. "And for God's sake, keep our secret."

Max did not reply incase any Farang might overhear a confirmation that he would need to justify in interlocution.

Max spent many ponderous days, wai-ing, and then being waid in return. Always a smile and eye contact, just like Glasgow. After a month Max kinda got why the scotts thought Londoners Bitches with a capital C. Saturday the fourteenth arrived sure enough. The journey was one of misdirection, first to Laxative city, since Dheli belly worked its magic on the flight, then a greyhound. His first contact. So frickin cheesy. Wearing a green beret.

"Senior, tienes fuego por favour."

"Lo siento, no fumar. Aber, Ich Spreche ein Bischen Deutche. Sprechen Sie Deutsche?"

"Sacre Coeures! Sept, Gouloise: Je n'cest pas por quois mais maintentant, J'aime ca!." His contact muttered.

"APK-CZY-DRN, O?"

A VW, Wagon pulled up sharpish. Possibly the only good thing Schickel Grouber ever pulled out of that God awful shitty mess. Yeah FUBAR!

"We've been informed by the Thai authorities you have the package."

"Yes, I have it, but first you need to prove something to me...as Max suddenly recognised an intense threat as they pulled away from the World Trade Center. "Wankers!" Thought Max. Can't they just go to a brothel to get a blow job. Why'd they wanna kick off a third world war. At least we've got trading places. At least. They can't destroy that living memory!" 5.

"You want money? We've plenty of that if you're as good as they say you are."

"You've just failed my test, drop me off at the next Grey Hound, and a five thousand dollars for my time."

WTF went through his head. What have I said?

Max guessed what he was thinking... "It's what you havn't said....yet. One more chance. I'll give you a hint...from where have I recently departed to land at LAX."

The analysist leapt into life..... "Compassion."

"A superb beginning to what I hope will be a lasting and warm professional relationship. My IQ is 768, My EQ is 3452 and My D7 is off the chart, Even the Zeeta chart, for example, will you kill me if I said to you right now, if you do not, they'll strike again? No, I didn't think so, it didn't even enter your head because you want something from me. It's the intention see, your desire for knowledge is blinding you to the possibility I suggested, for, within your subjectivity, how do you know? I fit the description yes, I am an hypnotic expert, or at least by abductor could be. Neither of you know for sure. Now ask yourself, 'how do I know this truth I am so sure of"

"Fair point" said the lanky analyst with fair hair.

Max wondered why analysts always tended to be a bit lanky.

"Now, compassion is, where is this package. Is it here in the Big Apple?"

Zeus was, again, mildly impressed that Mr Lanky paused between Now and Compassion

"Have you not heard a word I've said, I am the package. I can track anything and anyone. I am the worst nightmare for your enemies and I am as faithful as a Cocker Spaniel. But if for one moment you generalise Iran with Persia I'm out, that, my friend is my only condition."

Before Fuego man tried to respond, Mr Lanky, mouthed in the corner of Max's eye…. "We understand, yes, we admit, we racially profile, and I trust you to tell the difference."

"The Persian peoples must survive. The Kurds, must survive. We all must survive." Said Max, killing the period.

This author could tell you about the life of intel, dead drops, live drops, fear in your enemies eyes poop drops, but then again, as they say, I'd have to kill you. I could track you down through any one of the numerous bar code source code, interrelate purchase habits, and like a python, I'll simply drop from a tree and over the course of a day swallow you whole. Keep me all topped up for several months.

Hee Hee. ☺

Several months later, after returning from an Kaliningrad Oblast, after having an NVBD at Rotten Park road, because the pressure got too much…always a missing child…the hunter killer life, tracking the enemy and posting evidence to New Scotland Yard… Max just said it was due to excessive meditation, which was, no lie, but, being precise, was hardly the truth either.

In the once joyful kitchen of the student house something went rotten. The rabid dog came leaping to the surface with the pulsing arch of a greyhound. Thoughts of biting teeth, and then, yes, the teeth. 'Teacher', max thought, 'I wanted to bite it, but I was too scared, I was so afraid, he said he'd kill my sister. I'm so ashamed.'

The touch of buds to a strange leathery flesh was the seed of both an awakening to the cause of war, and, to find that cause not in a mortar shell, or the bastard wooden fuckers that the mine detectors couldn't...pick up, but the positively wanky nobends that wasted their time watching the news and feeling so powerful that they knew that this crime was the cause of the destination of the shell to find each other. The shell finds its destination by destroying the friend who is also unaware that the Nazis were quite simply, Paedoze; as my father explained to me in a language only a father can bequeath to a son at 11 years, on 10 mile hikes through the Water Ford country side. Fording the rivers of grandfather's stories. Zach became aware in the depths of the Azimuth, as he enjoined conversation with the scum of the earth, that their life, or lack of it, had a language all of its own. A backwards logic that sucked you in the moment you tried to apply The Logic Book. Like the dark web, their web of lies became truth as they envied one another if the other had a greater evil.

Sharing a joke in real happiness, I wish I could be as cruel as you, but its such hard work, our way of life, isn't it. A thankless task that the evil people piss away their lives trying to be polite and courteous.

Interim Position

This story began to find the child within. Zach had a son and his mother sang his lullaby. The first stanza of book one was embedded with an enslavement. To be enslaved to a quiet violence of my child, to which, to this day, the boy within no longer asks why, for the touch of tongue to a strange flesh. No longer feeling pity for that monster of a human being. The horizons of a future for the next fifty years. Flute, drums, an interest in mathematics and physics. A mind full of answers and a beautiful life yet to prove them. So, the demise of one's teacher, being, parents, peers or life, was, as it was, a suicidal preoccupation to escape the chatter of my own tongue. If you're out there, hold on...please. There is a life you are unaware of, full of wonder. It doesn't matter how you define your beliefs, yet, a few simple sentences ain't gonna cut it... as we both know. Book two, opens up on to a vista of exploration. Scientists call God wonder, A Buddhist master once said to me that God is a Mystic, BUT what matters to me, is that, if you have touched as I have, please....hold on. Shall I continue? Yes, I think I shall...

BOOK 3

The Fourth Element of Perfection

Abstract terror is as likened to the absolute silence at the very moment before the rabid spider squeals at the full-blooded moon. This was the statement and the question that occupied the Sajik. The Sajik peoples' cultivated understanding was such that the individual was submerged in the continual development of communal thought, an excrescence of conception that fought against the limiting- belief that suffering was a concept eternally and inescapably manifest as a moment of unfathomable pain. The hyperonic war was the birthchild of aeons of physical conflict, defined by the Thed Sajik as Force Blinded by its Own Action, or FBOA, which kinda sounded like many decent acronyms; as an ancient township on the African subcontinent. The Thed Sajik, known simply as the Thed amongst the Sajik superclass, were an antique demi-class within the Sajik hierarchy. Within the act the motivation becomes subservient to the victim's need to understand....why? This question, ***laid bare*** by the timeless longing for sentient meaning, asks in the chasm of unknowing – stop, I don't understand. But the word in the dark existence of nowhere never finds its voice. Thus, the slave to force sees only power. ***A strange kind of strength that desires to be cruel and knows it so.*** Of the worlds of the Thed that lived their short lives in the dark room two escaped, just two, and they passed on their secret knowledge and were the progenitors of the Hyperonic war. U. This was a war without force. The communities of the Thed lived amongst the Sajik. They lived as an example. Their training was torturous, and for a good reason. Self-defence as a psychological pattern of behaviour where they learned to navigate destiny with their feelings instead of manipulating the world around them. They certainly were not philosophical realists, although they knew the realist domain better than any other in the probable multiverse. For those who controlled the material sector, the concept of a world existed in itself, independent from observation. The Thed resisted, with unreasonable emotional recognition, to grasp the world with the mind. Instead, it was a part of the fabric of their larger reality, utterly existent and sometimes, *utterly alone.*

THE STORY OF THE ESCAPE OF THE TWO THED SAJIK

Noesis and Taqua had both been created in standard form. They were just two amongst the six million new lives commissioned by the Council of Equitable Value: The CEV. They were to develop on the new territory recently formatted for survival. It was designated Sector 7.81 in probable existence 4.397URG4222. Although was called home, just Home, to those who were about to develop and live there. The 800 million or so life trajectors worked on the inner and outer mechanics of fields such as: Id disturbance factors within the kinaesthetic limbic system, conceptual imagination influence on propositional inference, empathy transference, abstract logic decompression rates post physical time travel on two levels: one across the Heisenberg brane to formically near identical parallel universes, and the other to divergent universes; hormonal relevance in case of mind dislocation tolerances, and the like, as well as bog standard issues such as: fear dampening and such implications for long term social stability. Pretty standard in their timescale. In all there were approximately 200 trillion variables, trailing off into unknown interference parameters that numbered in the region of a google to the googleplex. The vague trajectory of this new civilisation was calculated within a reasonable tolerance and the lives were sequenced and grown, together with the run of the mill technological enhancements. The CEV ran a secret protocol for this batch, one that could be easily overlooked in the diversity of creation; the triune of emotion, recognition, and instinct was given over to autonomous control....to just two. If physical conflict erupted along their shores of safety, the inevitable would happen. The spiders were so strong, *just so strong*, in psychic ability, and, physical impenetrability. And the two would be taken into their darkness just like the rest. With all the sophistication of all that could, and some things that could not be conceived three things still survived unchanged in fundamental essence from the home of all homes, Erith, as it was niw named: The propensity and susceptibility to pleasure and pain, and the Heisenberg uncertainty principal. Well that was the sense of humorous import anyway. When things went well they praised the Pacific, when things went wrong they blamed the Sun, and when they got lost in probable space they cursed Heisenberg.

The CEV were themselves a hidden organization, in plain sight. Their language was as old as Erith itself, this phrase had a different meaning from when the Sun went red giant. It was composed of the type of people you read about but never meet. Except, when making their clandestine acquaintance after over-hearing the worst joke you ever heard at the next table, reminding you of when sheep went Baaaa, cows went Moo, pigs went Oink, ducks went Quack and then wondering about giraffes.

Spartac's and Seshan's Degrading Entanglement

"Dad, what's a Quack?" Spartac asked of his father.

Xerxes gave out a breath of laughter. He glanced to Asal and said, in his inimical way that never talked down to children,

"A quack is a pejorative term for a doctor of the mind. It's also how ducks communicate."

"Do Quacks quack?"

Xerxes thought intensely for just a moment.

"If you need a Quack, they can help you quack."

"But I talk."

"That's exactly what Quacks are for."

Xerxes knowingly slipped in the word 'pejorative' so the meaning would stick and the context would explain itself. Spartac never asked anyone what pejorative meant again.

The Second Element of Perfection

There were four elements of perfection. In a Dose – the morpheme they used to denote an aggregate of some kind of intense complexity; contradictory universes, paradoxical non....time travel, the simultaneity of individual and group identities, stuff like that - the CEV had discovered those very four. The Sajik and, unbelievably so, even the Thed did not know the origin of the four elements. The Sajik, in everyday commerce with the Thed simply believed some folk a long time ago meditated, perhaps on a sleepy paddy hill, or studied ancient scriptures, or met some guru in beaten-track village and oke up or realised something deep and profound about God or gods, or something or other. But the Sajik answered these questions with their wise ignorance and they did not lie. Amongst the Thed their training was first, not lie, secondly not to lie even at the risk of their own life, thirdly they taught that they did not know how to teach the ignorant path. And primarily, it was ordained by the punitive decree of astonishingly bad death-breath that if a Thed thought up a crap joke they must tell the closest person to them however humiliating it might be.

These four axioms constructed a mindset that was blinded by the very blinding instigation of FBOA. The Thed just told the truth. These were the elements of perfection they lived by: The first element of perfection was the Bumble bee. The second element of perfection was Monastic Bull Frog. The third element of perfection was any one of the Cows in Dharamsala, India. The fourth element of perfection was the joy of over hearing someone ask in a casual, ordinary, in one of those Yaaay! Kind of days – wondering.... "What's Love?"

A Long Time in the Future, Somewhere Far Far Away

Precisely 299792458 million Erith years from the CEV commission woman Music asked of woman Ethereal, as they sauntered past a bunch of tangerines debating upon the entropy of shirts,

"Have you ever thought it odd that the Thed couldn't teach the ignorant path."

To which Ethereal stated.

"No. They were ignorant and they knew it."

"How'd you know that, my lipstick's pretty ignorant but I wouldn't say it was wise."

"I never said your lipstick was wise."

"Going by your logic we may as well ask those tangerines out on a date. I recon I'd get more sense out of a tangerine. At least they know what shirts are......I think."

"Ok, I concede, I give you a little latitude, yes, the wisest progenitors of our subsequent history occasionally talked utter bollocks."

"You're going to say it aren't you, your perennial question...."

"Yeah, so how does an ignorant Thed disappear into the unknown of their own ignorance. Where the hell did they go?"

"Disappeared up their own tangerine probably. Yeah, the greatest gift they could give us they gave,

Language....but by heck sometimes tangerines really do do my Ed in."

The Council of Equitable Value

The protocol was initiated by a wise nobody: Spartac, in Earth time 2014. The question he asked, as the Thed pawed over the badly corrupted metta-data drawn from the empathy field, not an easy thing to do over such a distance of time, was, is the immeasurable suffering of one justified to save two from what he could only call…. 'the monster'. The CEV considered leaving Spartac alone in the memory of time, because 'the monster' was, for him, crippling to confront. However; compounding the life force of his thought, even though it could and possibly would, dig up his grave, was necessary to them. Thus, there were two risks at either end of time, his peace in his death and their survival. In the timespan the Thed wished to unearth, this was his choice that they would become part of: if Spartac succeeded but failed to find the end of eternity, he and his sister would survive, but the pain would never end, and his sister would never be aware that he had not returned. The CEV found an answer for him, a little too late mind you, but they did do some justice to his anonymity. The unfathomable pain could be everything in such a state, if there is nothing that is not pain, then, since they knew that philosophical concepts, all of them, were still subject to relativistic rule, then in that condition pain is not relative to the relativity – ***there is no pain because everything appears to be precisely what it is.*** The CEV needed that which was lost to Erith time, lost when Spartac died his spectacular death; the moment he found the ropes he consciously dropped when freestyling on that monumental cliff face, as he began to scream LO.., as a rabid wolf ripped off his lower jaw. They needed the secret he died with. They did not know it yet, but the secret he had was their very name. The Thed did not know their names, for that was part and parcel of their ignorance. They knew that the recognition of emotion may have the meaning necessary to defeat the ferocious intellect of the spider race. Emotional recognition, so experimental they gave it to just two, Noesis and Taqua. Noesis designed to be a heterosexual man and Taqua similarly designed to be a heterosexual woman. Intersexuality was more a form of expression at Erith than a drive to creativity, although creativity was by no means limited in intersexuality. Life was still life, and death still a certainty, except Taxes were now just a chance to laugh about the past, as they handed their children fairy money.

THE EL CONTINGENT

The CEV named the emotional recognition "The EL contingent". For, over the vast expanse of time that *forgetting became necessary to survive*, the concept Spartac found that the CEV recovered could only be deciphered as "EL". It was a tragic yet triumphant concept.

Something to do with the unconditioned. Even the CEV, in all their pomp and circumstance, found it funny that the Buddha did not use hair conditioner, since, he had no hair. That he was, in fact, unconditioned. Consequently, a group of three CEV suffered from a month's long death-breath after they told that semblance of a joke to a group of descendants of Burmese lizard loungers in Nepal. These place names were the closest match to archaic history that he CEV could make out, so, antient monuments and cities became the go to places. For example, the Pogo-Stick emporium in Addis Ababa was actually THE place Confucius liked to hang out in the afterlife. A gin joint of ill repute where Lau Tzu was definitely not. Ha! Shortly after contracting the breath when they asked those descendants for directions to the nearest PSE. Their breath mocked the air like a bad dream and the entire area was modified for chemical reconditioning.

JUST TWO

Just two individuals amongst several billion, by the time - population growth, would never be detected, if, as it was the case, the variables of emotion recognition would be only a couple of billion to a google to the googleplex. The CEV, debated in Dissonance Logic for several years in a closed assembly before the commission of Home, and, subsequently, concluded that it was necessary to partially pre-empt an entire world for the purpose of war; a retaliatory incursion. Noesis and Taqua would be protected on the front lines, in their estimation in a war commencing in two thousand years, they would be taken to the rooms to die, however, in that room *Noesis and Taqua could survive* through *emotion recognition* and bring back the knowledge of what actually happened in the rooms.

What happened where their psychic machines could not penetrate, where something sacred was taken. It was a gamble because there was something missing from the equation: how to find an end to the eternal moment. But in Earth time, Spartac had the answer before he died. If they brought his living knowledge into their time, they would do exactly what this ancient progenitor of their philosophy denied them do; they would have to relive his unspeakable past as they formed psychic union with the meaning of his existence. Spartac specifically stated, his last words, written and sent to the Bull Frog in Chiang Mai: 'Never dig up my grave – you would not survive, and, you would break the heart of your best friend.' The CEV tried, at first, instead, to find the Bull Frog Monastery but the monks' telepathic communicae were too well suppressed. The CEV went cold and clammy at the thought of possibly breaking their best friend's heart. It was a choice. Defeat the spider race, or, defeat their friend. *That's what the spider race forced them into.* An impossible choice, and their intellects fed off the expelled emotion as the Sajik and many other races died alone in the rooms, asking just before the very moment the spider wanted, the moment after they asked ….. 'why?'. So, logically, in logical consideration of the form that war takes, they chose to defeat their friend and the spider race. They would ask Spartac the secret and Noesis and Taqua may be able to return to Gaia Central Point with the knowledge of the moment; the moment just after the spiders would have them murdered.

THE OVERHANG: EARTH TIME

Fist grip! That's all Spartac could think as he dangled there under the overhang with his fist firmly lodged in the crack of the granite seam. Your fingers might break if you wait another hour. Don't even think about it. Logic. Concentrate. It is the parameter of this ineluctable circumstance that there is no choice. Do not therefore think of the future. Meditate, remember the chedi. Glasgow University, geology, fault lines, obsidian, concoidal fractures, strata, anything please, the fuck come to mind. Intuition. Use your ff....calm. Use the living rock as the programming of your neurolinguilism. Lingual, his body reacted to the living Rock, as Sitting Bull sat: Mother earth. Mother of us all. Splendid as Rock. 'All Spartac could think of was, "MF, Mother of eff all, Hard as Fuck! Home, I must get home." Intuition is related to both fear and sensibility, therefore, modal logic - normative ethics.

Calm. Shit. What if drop. My friends. They'll never make it. Why did you drop your effing ropes. For a god damn laugh cos you wanted to live at the edge. Lost your mind cos o' some crazy holy man's prescient advice. Shit, member now, said make a choice between abstract fear or a gift from a holy man from Rajastan, as the joint lit up his orange glow in the mountain lion woods. Glad I gave him my sax....damn, focus, I'm going nuts with fear. Regret it now, don't you....idiot! Use the fear of the demise of those you Love, channel. Got it. There's a basalt strata. I should have payed attention. Articaria, nightlong itch. Doctor. Skipped that lecture. Damn articaria. I don't know fuck all about how to read these strata. There's always some kind of hold, but where? What if I snap my hand as I flip round. Yeah that might work. NOW! Don't even think about Zen, just do....!

Empty Air

In a moment out of time Spartac's head rounded the curve, his wrist snapped, fingers following. He even had the awareness to think, 'thank fuck for that' as he arched through the empty air. Somehow his instinct capitulated with the rock face, he had a hold. He knew, from experience, he had about fifteen minutes before the oxygen debt. For some reason Spartac at that point could've really used a rollie as he hung there. No chance. One hand and no footing. I think this predicament is precisely the reason why the phrase 'I'm totally fucked' was invented. I can't even have a rollie before my arm gives out…Fuck. Spoze I'll think up something to put a smile on my face before the inevitable. Well, that's one lesson that won't come in useful, learning to roll with one hand from that gangster in Bangkok. Beautiful man. You can't judge the covering of one's body simply because of the B tat his entire Platon."I don't know who you are or where you come from but no one in a thousand years has rounded to our village."

UNPHASED

Unphased Spartac replied, just after he concealed his note of a small Psi tattoo on this man's lowered upper forearm. Thinking with a borrowed strength, boy he'd pay for that with a headache later, rapid machine gun fire of propositional logic to stimulate spontaneous memory. The Psi Symbol, yes, England, Guy's hospital. A clunky fella by the name of, I think, no the name escapes me, gave me a detailed map of gathered intelligence of a Hospital called Guy's that he used to escape. Told me about western symbols. Yes, a close Fit, Psychology. What's clinical psychotherapy got to do with him. Oh shit, he must be the Emperor. I've trespassed. I'll have to offer him my life. Custom in this part of the world is such an offering of his very bed, but by law he could just as easily take my life. Never happens, just a nuance of some ancient custom. Bus still, a tad intimidating that it's in black and white. I can't even think about not offending a Psychiatrist, I have to change myself or something. Damn this is scary. Oh yeah, I'm still hanging here. Gotta come out of non-time soon. Persian hospitality must have been here at some point in history. That hospital. Their discipline. I never did discover how they trained.

They didn't sit for three days to get that pain control. Maybe it's secret. I suppose that would make sense, since as Socrates pointed out, a physician's knowledge in the wrong hands can do a lot more harm than good. They healed the sick on an industrial scale. Zoot at base camp just wouldn't believe a word. Good on an industrial scale. I've heard it all now."I could use a hand, cos, like, mine's totally…. 'polity...polity, potentially a new friend, now's not the time to ask his name, you need focus for that' ….broken."

"Ha, ha…..got yourself in a pickle eih. We've got a few minutes to figure this out. Stay there."

"Oh don't make me laugh….this really isn't the right time."

"mmmm, I've a scarf in my bag. About 9 seconds to say the following, ten seconds to remove it in 7 seconds time. About 37 seconds to wrap it around your wrist, if you can raise your arm?"

'ffffffffffffffffffff' "Yeah no problem."

"Why are you telling me it's not a problem. Just raise your arm."

"Like this."

"Yes plonker, like that."

After a few wasted seconds they had the scarf tightly wrapped with three reef knots, quick and effective. The knots tightened on themselves as Spartac's weight gave the pressure. The man wrapped the end of the scarf around his wrist and pulled with a consistent strength, then, rather ungracefully, Spartac slid onto the shelf completely oblivious to his mangled hand. A modicum of pain control is in order here, he initiated already, an hour ago.

He looked up.

"What, what are you doing here? I thought this was a plateau." As he surveyed the false summit.

"All in good time. First, we've got to figure some stuff out. Are you hungry, you'll need your strength!"

"How many hours climb from here?"

"About three weeks."

Spartac swooned as he nearly lost consciousness with the untenable strain upon hearing that, and a small yet potent dose of PTSD. Mostly what was really going on in his head was....I can't believe it, you've saved our **Life**, I don't think you understand the magnitude of the heartfelt gesture of humanity. So many lives depend on me making it. Oh, why did I drop those ropes. - Giving in to natural language and feeling *shame*. - Idiot, he's a supremely intelligent and confident man. He can no doubt figure out exactly where I've come from, from the dialect of ancient Sanscrit on my headscarf. Oh no. Don't tell me he knows that. I can't keep a secret from a doctor. This is a most testing situation. For change, I ain't backed against a wall with rabid dogs snapping at my feet. He'll know how to navigate exactly what he can see. What is expected of me**?** That is my question.

When he came round he asked again, "Please kind Sir, how may I address you?"

"I'll tell you what, as we ascend, we can play a little game of try and guess."

"But, in my trai….."

Spartac remembered, startled he even uttered 'trai', the secret his teacher taught him never to reveal.

"I need to be respectful to you Sir, I'll call you Sir."

"Wrong, hee hee."

"I need to call you something, I'm confused, what if I fall or something and need to call out your name."

"Just shout….ssssshhhhhhhiiiiiiiittttttt!"

"But that would be disrespectful." His new friend was totally impressed with that answer, but not as impressed as Zeus.

Spartac, remembering his training, he recalled the penultimate conversation with his master.

ZACH AND HIS AJAHN

'Always ask a new friend's name.....politely. Look into the meaning that word gives them. This will tell you what they search for, for all people need their name. A name is always given, and, in the exchange of a wider cultural context, that which is given is also lacking. Not because their heart is not strong, but because, in their name, they love their given gift of that name, and they search to give that gift back to the world. The world can be cruel, and this they need to give is often an unrequited love. Our secret is that we can provide the answer to a person's name. Tell no one of our secret civilisation. No one will ever understand that we know what perfection is, and, more than that, even a good man may defend his name with his life. If they discover that the perfection they do not know they seek to give to their friends is the name that you know better than they know themselves, with the best intentions you will be ostracised from every warm home, every warm fire and every warm conversation. When you leave the walls of this monastery, you must live the rest of your life never to teach this training, however desperate the plea, however confident the student. Along the way, give good people the perfection of their name.'

'How will I know if they love Bumble Bees?'

'Tell them about Monastic Bull Frog. If they smile, they love Bumble Bees. Do not reply after I tell you this, just turn and walk away……you will meet a Sadu in the north, India, at the foot of the Lamas' new home, tell him from me, this is India, as vast the Caucases' eagle, as deep as Marianas trench. Make the connection and let him teach you the meaning of God: tell him from me that The Bull Frog's path, our Bull Frog, eventually culminates in relinquishing evidence in favour of a subjectivity naked before the desire to find a meaning that can sustain itself in the experience of time.

Sit and let Sitting Bull tell you your name.'

Spartac's diaphragm lurched but he suppressed the urge to blurt…. 'After all we've been through don't you think I know *my name* by now', but he just turned.

SPARTAC TAKES T BY THE HAND TO THE LAND OF PSI

Spartac lay on his front peering over the edge with a thick stomach whilst his new friend collected Osprey eggs further up the cliff face. Not a hard climb. Just an easy chimney. The clouds made a mirage of his memory of Zoot.

"Eat these", he said as he returned to Spartac, "get some rest".

Spartac lunged with spasms into the well of his sleep.

He dreamt, predictably, about the moment he chose to drop his ropes. Just a kind of a quiet feeling as he thought.... 'Belief, who needs belief when the obtained is not sustained by the changing mind, but God this is for you, because I know what you mean, for those who need, those who have gone beyond the implication of matter, and those who know, '..... then let go and shouting 'siiiiiiiiiiit', waking up to being shaken vigorously at the shoulders by his new friend.

"Wake up, wake up, sharp, we have a break, ten minutes, no more, to get through that crack before the magma wells up again and the heat drives us back. It's a one off for sure, this hardly ever happens. It's a day's walk along the cavern arete. Once we're through to that ledge, we're home and dry, well, with your hand, a problem but nothing we can't handle. Then we can have tea. By the way, that's my name....Te."

Spartac's eyes shot wide. It was the way he said it.

"errr", trying to be casual, "what kind of Tea". Completely forgetting that he could well be the Emperor. He suddenly came to his senses. The facts are I am at ease in his company. I better not assume that that my death is his intention. I'll just go with it. Maybe he sees danger and he's just getting us out of here to safety quick.

"You know, the usual, taste of Dhamma."

'He could have heard the phrase somewhere', Spartac thought.

"With a little honey of course." He added.

That did it. The taste was one thing. But Asal was quite another, Asal, his mother's name, meant 'honey' in Persian.

"Quack quack.....quack." Té voiced.

Spartac couldn't help himself as he skipped to keep up....he asked, softly, almost inaudibly 'you knew my mother?'

"Knew it was you. You're the conceivable one. Yes, one bright afternoon seven years ago I heard a voice in my head. I thought. Now this is very unusual. It said, quite oddly........from now on put honey in your tea. I drank it up and the warmth of the of the water filled my blood. I felt a word embody me like another body, and a beautiful spirit became inextricably and a part of me. So, Honey was your mother?" He said rhetorically. "She told me you would come, and, for some reason, that she would always be in my tea. Perhaps the afterlife has got a thing for sweet beverages?"

"Yes, Honey was her Persian name. She passed into memory of those she loved seven years ago"

....then the flood gates opened. He turned and put his back against the wall and slid down the rock, sat, cradling his head Spartac sobbed, connected to this man and completely unaware of the motivation behind any potential discourse. Then said confidently, with an intermittent voice, and **tasting salt.**

"I was taught to let everything in and fight my own defence. When I defend myself I don't know who I am."

Te crouched flat feet firm on the ground, then extended his neck a little and calmly said with a firm voice full of character:

"God shines bright in the night,
But day after day,
day arrives with a break,
Matter matters not for the hydrogen fright,
The impermanence of the largest star,
In time a still lake.

…come I'll show you the Lake of Hubris when we arrive home."

Spartac was touched that the absence of the pronoun implied a mutual home. Mi casa es su casa. Crepusculo es Bueno, no?

Seshan Discovers Star Wars

For the next week, and a few tricky spots, Spartac and Té chatted like they'd been best mates for many, many years. Spartac flung the secret into the air. His teacher had finally got through to him. He found a man, an ordinary man, with extraordinary understanding, someone who could tell him exactly how to cope with his father's grief. No one would understand, except Te, so those years betwixt father and son went unwritten. Something to do with Ozwiecim when tears run barren, oneself empty of expressed grief and yearly finding the strength, father, then son, to expel the tears that really belonged to the frame closely wrapped in sepia skin. No diary. Neither he nor his father believed in diaries. Making a nice little note of an observation of a conversation wasn't gonna stop the Iran Iraq war. So many relatives hanging in the balance. As his father taught him at an extraordinarily young age, making him a man way before his time, he said to Max "The difference between a man and a boy is that a man allows himself to contemplate the implications of war, a child lives your very real world of existential freedom." Spartac's training was even beginning to unravel, which all his masters from the four corners of China articulated, was an impossibility. Could he tell him about the empty diaries?

No! Was a sudden answer demanded, no, ordered, with a commander's bark straight from his **H**eart.

'My master must have known.' Said Spartac to himself as the brow of the hill at a week's end walk yielded its horizon to reveal what his eyes disbelieved. There were monumental structures, the most grand structures he had ever seen towering into the stratospheric clouds. He could make out tiny floating capsules. Colours were abundant. Extravagantly sculpted contours of a new city that arced and weaved like water.

Spartac considered further: 'How did my master bring me here, to this man, to complete my training. He always did say, 'Only through friendship will you find you need not have learned that which we are about to teach.' 'One day, let go' were the first words he heard his master say over his shoulder within the monastic circumference. 'He must have known that I sought only to be student. And now I have discovered that friendship has no master. This man, Te, has shown me enlightenment and it has little to do with understanding, it is the gift of a friend. Two people, incipiently unknowing of the life they search to connect to, make a journey of thought to the edge of their experience, then meeting, the realm of the unknowing of another's subjective abundance is constant, and constantly they can learn, discovering each other, they are not alone. The question they could not ask, is answered by the act of faith, to learn about each other. A level of existential awareness, elevated from the heartache of concentration. A pain where pain was not allowed to live. *The confiscation of acknowledgement for evil's purpose*. The decimation of interpersonal relativity, forcing into the minds of the subjugated an impression of evil that their hearts were maliciously decerebrated to fight. Spartac found a friend, leading him to the Shangri la of discovery. He wondered if his friendship, as little as he thought it was, was enough for Te. Perhaps he saw the depth as he did, that, to find each other we find the complexity of death, and also the lives he and his father wept for. Life did not find its own cure. It was not a lugubrious God that gave meaning, but a God that required work upon work to discover life's secret. Max's own little journey to find Nietzsche after syphilitic insanity. Each other, in life as in death.

As Spartac joined Té along his path, the grass slowly began to become earth. The miles stacked upon themselves and Spartac's neck craned to see the heights of these foreign structures. Then, Spartac's head turned to leave the momentum of his brain behind. Just as quickly Té turned to him and said... "So, you remember your name?"

"Holy Sh....I mean....Big pile of Bee poo! I'm from a village in a place called Chonbury in Thailand.

The Waterfall, I remember now. The blasts of wind I wondered where all the air came from, being sheltered on all steep sides. I think, I think that was my first memory. I was with Maha Pizzit, my father, he said to me the first words I ever understood – Khun Santiparp Krup. This translates into this dialect we share as – peaceful man.

These vehicles that move like bullet ants in the sky, they're reminding me of the stories I heard about in a place called England. Sky wars, star wars, or something like that. I remember teaching a man called Spartac about the concept I travelled with from Thailand, isotropic space. He said that we could exchange personas with his technology. I have within me still something called an Intertwined quanta"

"What's a quanta?"

"Something so small it can only be seen by other quanta."

"Oh, you mean particle! An entangled particle. There's plenty of them by the lake of Hubris. So you say, you exchanged who you are with one another with this technology. We're advanced here sure, but I've never heard of that. England you say. Interesting."

"Yep, It was a favour to him. He needed time. That's it. He said, there would be a place that their diamond spheres had detected but could not locate. This is that very place I believe. I don't know what happened to him but the concept you need. You need a concept do you not. This is why I'm here. My name is Seshan, and I have the concept of isotropic space!"

“Big pile of Bee poo indeed! You remember. If you hadn’t **had** remembered of your own accord the concept may have been lost. It’s the last piece. It’s complicated, but it’s needed by the future. The entropy of shirts sustains a possible reality with language. Pardon me, the future is oft difficult to read, I mean, your concept, the concept of isotropic space is needed by future humanity, to defeat the legacy of war.”

“It’s simple, said Seshan, it’s the absence of the concept of existence.”

“Quiet!” said Te.

“There’s a reason that your identity was hidden, even from yourself. The secret remains. When we arrive by the lake, I’ll tell you how we can use your experience of this absent concept, but still, I know you are bursting with the exploration of your memories, but there are only four that can know this experience of yours.

You, me, and Noesis and Taqua.

Spiritual Evidence

Seshan had all the evidence of two years, nineteen hours a day, delaying the agony of lotus for a kind teacher's words in each morning where the twilight of his mind became the twilight of finding his stumbled sleep-deprivated way across the courtyard to breakfast with the nuns and monks. Spiritual evidence was difficult to define – it was a sprinkling through the single moment of two years – of feelings and symbols of a deep union – Té smiles – he would have loved that frog as much as he did. Secret. There were three things his teacher said that cannot remain hidden for long: the sun, the moon, the truth. Except the Bull Frog was not a secret for the symbolic evidence was captured between Seshan and his teacher the moment Gaia opened the Amazonian rivers to his heart. Besotted in a spiral of negative space; Seshan worked hard as Humanly possible to submerge that Single moment, giving perfection to the frog and wishing him a: most moist mosquito munching mood.

THE MONASTIC BULL FROG

Seshan contemplated that if he were handed a gun he would have seriously contemplated rapidly dismantling his brain, the food was that hot! One of the nuns pointed - Seshan didn't look up, timid for the disrespect of libidinal disturbance to her sensitive practice - to different foods on the tray, and as Seshan ate them in sequence the pain abated. Coup Khun Mai Krup....were the words he was with most familiar, as he said to his teacher each morning.... thank you very much. He took a last slurp of soya milk and went out to the courtyard that was greeted with the accustomed yet freshly enlightened warmth, the mosquitos were napping, having had their breakfast too, after the morning dusk. Seshan truly loved to see such a precarious creature land on his arm. Absent minded to malaria he let it have breccy on him. He gave a little of his heart to the mosquito because Mrs Webster in class 4 said, sometimes the little things are more important than the big things. Later he would reflect on that and get all paranoid. Something unspoken spoke to his wonder, a frog. A big, fat, frog. Just sitting there. But it didn't just sit. It seemed to know exactly what it was. Yes, I am a frog, it said. So what? I know what I am, don't you know what you are, it seemed to say. But not in a way that was condescending. It was a jovial knowledge that just ate mosquitos, occasionally. And it just sat there, with a stolid vestibule of a body. Plump, yet firm. As Seshan slowly approached the frog he wondered if it would hop away, but no, it didn't budge a confident inch. Seshan crouched down but his heels were high, painfully reminding him of how he envied the Thais who could crouch for hours on end, preparing a meal with their feet firmly on the ground. He envied how Mai Chi Pit could sit and contemplate emptiness for three days straight, no food and no water. In the morning she would be at the temple door, in the evening she would be at the temple door, and the following morning followed by another evening and yet another. Maybe she was the frog. Then, as Seshan's eyes were transfixed by the silent pure happiness of this creature an arm stretched out over his left shoulder. It was understood between this hand and the frog and Seshan that there was something special about this moment. The hand clasped the frog behind its pelvic girdle. It lifted the frog without so much as a glimmer of a struggle, turned, and placed the frog back down. Why didn't it hop away? The teacher was close. Morning after morning Seshan only wished to a be student and the teacher could not find him. Where was the teacher in the student that only wanted one question answered. How do help my father? We know of unanswerable suffering, and we cannot help each other for the world is endless. Concentrate, his teacher would say. Seshan found the first form of concentration he had ever trusted. The frog's kind. He stretched out his hand as he still felt the presence of the arm, he clasped the frog behind the girdle, lifted it, turned it back to its original position and placed it down. Normally Seshan would have been afraid that the frog would want to hop away from the moment, but he was just happy the froggy was willing to play, or at least tolerate his company. Probably had better things to do, like, dunno, croak or something. You are his son, the monk said. I am the frog's son, Max thought. Between them, all three of them, the purpose of Buddhism had fulfilled its promise to a child, but a little too late. A painful lesson exiting his teens – life's no fairytale. His father, unknownst to him had died like a lion the day before, many, many miles away. Seshan thought later, when learning this, that he was too late, that he could have given the natural world, the frog, to his father. But his teacher, taught him, to find a true friend, that could help him let go of concentration and experience his father in the nature of the world he was now a part of. I'm so fucking sorry, were the words his heart said, if it could speak, and one day....it would. Should have paid closer attention to the five precepts. Shot back three double whiskies and pissed his life away as he hit his father. The previous morning as Seshan was working on his Prince in the ten minutes before breakfast, he translated goodbye from Chinese, a bookshelf with a T and a roof with two streams. He was forgiven within the bidtheefairwell and fairwellibidthee, schizoaffective disorder his father knew as Max read one of the many books in the library, "One cannot repay one's debt to one's parents. Stricken with inconsolable grief. "It's my fault, I precipitated the aneurism!"

Ajahn, withheld his tears for later, and said, simply "Your father was a good man, he loved you from the moment your mother said she was pregnant with YOU. This debt you do not need to repay, for when your eyes were bright, he would thank Sitting Bull, for the precious moments of joy you brought into his life."

"It's still my fault! He was my best friend, kindnesses and gratitude for my company since I can remember, and that's how I fucking repay him. Sorry for swearing master."

"I understand."

"Maybe if I leap from Chonbury waterfall, I can find him in the next life and try to explain something that'd make sense. It's my fault. I owe him my life. There's so much I havn't told you. You don't understand."

"Tell, what is it that I don't understand?"

"We shared the grief of the death camps. His spirit was barely holding on and the camps induced this insanity within me. I was barely holding on. It's my fault, because I loosened his grip on something he learned to trust in this shitty fucking world.....me!"

The Individuation of Spartac from Seshan

Upon remembering Oxhangweh Spartac became liberated spontaneously within his own unique consciousness from Seshan. The darkness had been awakened by my need to be completely free to see the truth of my father. He was a good man, good to the marrow of his bone. I see it with all the evidence of the relationships that sustain him in life. The way forward is, yet again, to let go of evidence and see this truth in the morning, in the afternoon and the evening. Man, looks like Seshan made it over the Wall Impossible, the entangled particles our mutual lenses have degraded spin now, or then, or, whenever. The negative space between us has now vanished, he must be free, god knows how that happened. It's been years. I've gotta deal with this now. My personality is so clunky. I must stick out like saw thumb amongst the smooth lost village emotions. Plonk me in front of my curving undulature and I could merge so well I could even supress Zenda's awareness. I mean man, what a bitch. If only I could have told tell her what I was planning. But, man, she would have given me straight away. Click clacking down the hall with that measured cautious tempo. Quathe would have spotted her straight off. And more than that, just follow her following me. And then bam. Back here with no credit. And then, after that, it would be my fault. She'd've blamed me either way. Had no choice. Sorry Zenda, Binary construction ain't exactly up there with zeeta decompression. Now that's exciting, actually being there when negative space collapses. Who would've guessed in the 21st century a philosopher could witness that. She always thought I was fucking around. And I just couldn't tell her. After our spat in the very first flippin day of induction all those years ago something great just got, spannered up. She had so much potential for lucid discourse. No, what am I thinking, she has such a lucid mind. The curvature's mood said we were a good match. But I'd've never've told her I used light to determine something so precious. Spoze it did it to us all. Hardly **anyone** had the energy left to last the journey. Hang, on. I'm getting it now. Spartac. Looking for the concept. Yeah. That beautiful kid I gave the water to. She gave me pure L.O.V.E. A little tiny concept that could so easily go amiss in the carbon monoxide smog. I made it, the crystal sphere's did their job. The models actually predicted that they would operate with such close tolerances. Panic. Passport. Yep. Concept with crystal chip. Oh yeah. Remember now, chips a bit fucked. How do I....no I'm not protecting this rectally. My gait would probably give me away. Gangster. Maybe.

What do I have to offer for his protection. Work. I'll see what's going. Ahh man. That's what to do with the concept. Something convenient, small and simple. Zenda and I could use it if I could get back. Oh. Firstly I've been travelling for **three** years as someone else. Even if I could figure out where the fuck I am and get back I'd have to be reinstated. I suppose I could **kill Quathe**, he is really irritating sometimes. No, seriously. How could I get reinstated after leaving the agency without permission. Prison time man. Not a cert but oh fuck. How does Love survive in this world. *I'll figure it out when I get there.* Save Zenda from binary construction with my knowledge of axiological ethics, she'd love me for that. Maybe she'd like to share it. Man, this is fucking out there difficult. On the one hand I'm contemplating servitude to some gangster, on the other hand I've a three year walk to Timbuku, all the whilst protecting this gift for a destitute child. This is getting a bit surreal now. Maybe if I got work I could save enough to post it. I wonder if they have a postal service wherever the fuck this is. Zenda, B-block binary construction. She must be going out of her mind with boredom. Well that's part of the job, interfacing with boredom itself. Once you're there they never move you up and you never move down. I'm such a bastard. It was the most convenient thing I could think of within the space of Quathe's remark that might get me to the concept. Well, at least her boredom is reliable. She would totes get that. That's why we had our spat.

All I said to the examiner was, negative Love can be used to acknowledge instinct which can protect positive love. I said to her, I understand why this seems unreasonable, I can see your point. But the southern hemisphere is so violent. Making our minds placid with fear. But we couldn't find middle ground and we never recovered. That could have been such an amazing working relationship. But no. Tick, tack, tick...........tack. I knew her tack. It was a, 'I didn't mean it but I'm still not backing down.' Well, anyway. I'm not asking her to accept that proposition. Just to recognise that child's gift and keep it safe for us till I get back. Man I'm worn out. I haven't thought like a computer for years.

Three to be precise. Yeah, why am I even contemplating. Even if I didn't ask. She'd instinctually find a safe place. Little does she know, I Love her. Mostly, I Love her because her proposition was far more direct than mine. But still, had a point. After that, man, so much more to do. Prison to avoid. Quathe to convince letting philosophers take, what seems something so utterly inconsequential, small, into the collapse of negative space. Well, philosopher's can be all, conclusion, but all the best are dead. Good old reliable Descartes. He broke out of the singularity and chose to trust God even though he damn well knew the argument he left behind was cyclical. I think he made it. They're all so, limit language nowadays. There was that Indian kid in, Crawley. His species inclined him to let go of publication so he could use the words every day as natural language. That's not genius. I know what that is. That's the predicament I'm in. He was fifteen, what, 12 years ago. Track him down. He, in my mind is a definite potential. Implying with his Kantian solipsism that love can form a structure with a distinct universe we call matter identical with the concept of the relationship identical to God. Separate and together, because many concepts match. Namely infinite numbers and fractional numbers. My heads spinning. No wonder he chose to let go of it. Wonder how he earns a living. Emotional recognition goes so far, but, I've, got, this.

Secret weapon.

L.O.V.E.

ZENDA DOIN HER NUT WITH BOREDOM

Zenda was indeed nearly going crazy with boredom. But then she spotted something that gave a little brightness in such a dull month. She noticed as the matrix streamed down the from the Architravian roof, something that repeated. That's peculiar. A repeating fragment. That shouldn't happen. R-168B. She wondered if this should be reported. Just more boredom to deal with. But she then considered those she was trying help at their ordinary jobs Tesco's, beep, beep, beep.

"Queef, I mean Quathe, you better get down here, I'm south of boredom. I've discovered repeating patters parked right in the middle of a byzantine piece of shit"

"Are you sure?"

"Apodeictic."

"I'll be there sooner than now."

Quathe arrived a little out of breath.

"See there it is again."

"That can't happen." Quathe said.

"Well it's happened, it's there plain as da....see there."

"Would you like this one Zenda."

"Oh Quathe, you are a dear. Please, please, give me a shot at Zeeta decompression."

"Well, okay, but only the negative parameters..... to start with eih."

"Oh Quathe, my savour from Binary construction."

Boson and Muon and succeeded in their mission.

ZACH S PARTICLE HAD BEEN DISCOVERED

"Wake up Boso, we've made it!"

"You're having muon."

Particle 3-gamma was small. I mean very, very small. It was his job to be small. That was what he did. He was the physical manifestation of the concept of the utterly minuscule. Instinctual recognition at the level of the odd undetectable muon sustained their questioning minds in the room. The pain does not render for any page, let alone this one, but the CEV found Noesis and Taqua, brutally tortured but their instinct kept their hearts alive. This was after the successful retaliatory incursion. Their hearts we're extracted and resequenced with a new brains, with their mind's pretty much as they had been for a thousand years, and the concept captured though schrodinger recognition by Zenda, recapitulated their union, and Taqua and Noesis were once more. They chose to live together despite painful memory, and their future was secure. The spider race would never curtail their shores of safety ever again.

GAIA CENTRAL POINT COMMUNICATING WITH ZENDA

Beyond the observable universe the civilisations that hung in the balance of probably existing succeeded. Someone's life had been changed for the better. The impossible still had not happened. The impossible: human culture of the future might be trying to give us the quantum coordinates. All anyone would have had to have done is cross reference R – 168B with the star charts. Such a long shot. The reality the future <u>culture of human **really** lived in</u> was like always living the knowledge: unknownst that you don't know where you are. And when they took the chance to communicate the quantum coordinates they became painfully aware that they might never have existed. This was the law of the pioneer. They were the only lives in the universe that had no home, yet thinking they were alive, didn't contemplate the possibility that they were lost, if, they chose to explore, the past.

The Place Everyone Knew of, Except the People Who Lived There

In a monastery in Tokyo, a monastery travelling so silently the Sangha did not even know where they were. Although, of course, the people who came with gifts of gratitude knew where they were. But the subject never came up so the Sangha continued living as they had always done without this knowledge, of which, If they had had known, wouldn't have changed things anyway. Except perhaps, as a Nun being told this knowledge could have brushed an unknownst spiders web in the corner behind her as she turned to say.....what?...and inadvertently freed a fly, that, in this hypothesis of: had the Sangha actually been told, the fly would have said 'Nice one Buddha, that fear was getting a bit tedious'.

Cut to eight years later, the Buddha arrived in the insight of a teenage boy recently ordained. The boy asked his teacher, after a week's stint of being a bit bored of trying to settle his mind down,

"How does a spider sit so still for so long?"

The Abbot of the Monastery replied.

"The spider is at one with its own nature. Oneness is an expression of a peaceful state of mind. This unity is a precious foundation for the rest of your journey."

"So, the spider is peaceful," replied Soupie. Then, disrespecting that which the teacher was about so say, he said sarcastically....so, "I suppose the spider's in Love too!"

Cut to five more years. Soupie chose to disrobe, as was the custom if the seat of the mind had any other commitments. He got fired from his first two jobs, for sleeping on the job and being constantly late. These were cooking Kau Pat Kai, succulent chicken with egg fried rice with a slightly tangy lemon-grass over-tone, in a Thai restaurant down-town, 24hrs 1 minute a day, but he did Love the food on his cigarette break, his favourite nosh. He didn't miss the lack of lack of sleep, but the morning endured for anticipation of heaven, if only for half an hour on his lunch break. The one thing in the entire island of need that made more sense than anything else. He loved his mum's chicken noodles of which he was reminded by Kau Pat Kai.

Te became destitute through sheer bad luck, so he chose to visit his parents on the island of Honshu, the drop from the Samurai sword, for one reason, to beg forgiveness. As he was stepping off the porch of his family house all those years ago Soupie's mother had ordered him to stay with family, so that he would support his pregnant sister with a fatherless child. When the escalation of tone became disrespectful his father stepped off the porch, light swinging, and grabbed Soupie's wrist. Soupie was so afraid, he had never seen his father like this and went to hit him. Struck in terror that he had transgressed the family line and then, wrenching his arm free ran into the night agonizingly relieved that he had missed.

The next morning, after awakening in a farang guest house, he thought, as he looked out of the window at a river snake dancing across the current. "I can't change what's happened, what's done is done. Nibbana will answer every question." So, he used his meagre savings to make it to the Buddhist master, the one his friend from school had told him could enlighten him as soon as he looked at him.

Soupie imagined wonderful stories about Nibbana, that it was perfect and you could have everything you want because you don't need anything. Soupie was determined to maintain the respect his father had taught him. He spent a month in the rain wondering whether, 'was all he wanted just a selfish desire for his mother's nosh, or, did he actually want forgiveness.' His parents brimmed over with an uncontrolled display of affection. Extended relatives were informed of his arrival. Everyone arrived quite briskly, you could say. There was food and celebration, and the familiar topics of conversation that Soupie had sadly forgotten in the years of morose self-absorbed need for the world to give him what he wanted. He had forgotten how a little shared memory can be so delightful. Sobbing, he asked his mother whilst they had a bit of alone time in the kitchen. A quiet kitchen, Soupie thought, was, basically unheard of in the Kodo family. Mother, I shouted at you, and nearly hit dad, I've disgraced the family. Then, still sobbing, he asked her......why do you Love me? I don't deserve your Love.

"Because our beautiful child, I have cried many nights wondering where you were, if you were safe, it is difficult to explain how deeply your father and I, God rest his soul, Love you. We Love you in the morning, we Love you in the afternoon and we Love you in the evening. Sometimes your father and I do not want the evening to end, because, what if we can't love you tomorrow. Feel these words, let them glide into your heart, and trust this simple fact, we love you unconditionally. Like a thick spherical glass container, containing super-heated plasma, something travelled into his heart. The glass shattered as it collided with the father of his sternum. He was convinced of something.

"Mother, I need to do something, I think it's important. The Abbot of a monastery, in Tokyo, I disrespected him. I need to tell him something. I'll probably be back by the end of next week."

Soupie got a little lost in the unfamiliar streets that only the inhabitants of Tokyo knew, as they pointed him to the place of which had no particular direction to speak of. He caught sight of the hem of his master's shoes as he vanished the corner of the chedi. Unmistakable shoes. So, Té thought, he ain't got a new pair for a mighty long while. Unless the Sangha buy all their clothes at the same outlet. Stop!

Shouted Soupie. Then looked around so see if he had disturbed anyone's concentration. The Master walked mindfully to Te, then, taking him by the hand said, "I have something to show you". They walked beyond the Chedi to the meditation hall. At head height, there was a spider's nest with a large neatly woven egg sack. "This spider sitting patiently in the middle. It has a family. Your father also had a family." Soupie replied, remembering with a solitarily brief agony of shame..... does it Love its family?" "You have been trying to find a place where you can forget where you've been and what you've done because everything reminds you of your father's Love. With that Soupie said. "<u>It's just unconditional</u> love isn't it, everything else kinds of all fits into place. My mother explained it to me last week." The master replied. "You are enlightened. Now, would you like some Tea?"

Over thick, salty buttered Tea the Master explained that Soupie's psychic abilities need to be controlled, and that he would show him the way.

Seshan, was startled out of sammadhi, when Soupie shouted 'Stop', the Buddhist version of smooth jazz, we're not talking Chet Baker, or even Miles Runs the Voodoo Down, but yeah, Ronny Scotts, best jazz club this side of New York. That's where my father introduced me to zoot suits and 20 minute drum solo's that knocked our socks off, so I always remembered after that first time to take an extra pair. Soupie is trying to find me and I'm in Sammadhi, beautiful sanctuary from a pain I just can't talk about. Gotta go, the Doc's brought lunch and another ream of plane paper. I asked for blank paper cos it's my second favourite object. Such infinite potential on a clean page. My favourite is my flute, Plaszy. The Doc asked me how things are going with Jawal? I said to him, she's so much more to me than that question. It's a bit of a drag sometimes being in in ward **seven,** just miss my flute. Oh, they let me play it, not all flippin day though. There's Jack, down the adjacent corridor. If I tell you he's good on the electric, he's good. Sometimes I stand outside his window in the rain just to listen. He's shy though, and doesn't want an audience. Plaszy is being re-padded at the moment. I'll pick it up day after tomorrow. Plaszy is her nick name. Plasma, is her official title. I'm such a selfish fuck, cos when I'm playing Plaszy I almost love her as much as Jawal, almost. Plaszy told me one day, "I'm a woman." When I was meditating with her. Just sitting with her and music in my iphone. And rollie, and a rollie and a rollie. Jazzzzzzz.

Spartac Meets Seshan

It was indeed a God forbidden send that Soupie shouted so loud. Not with his voice, but with his *emotion*. Seshan, accustoming his eyes from self-hypnosis raced to find the ocular junction so he could make out the man standing directly at his feet.

"There's no time, Spartac said. No pleasantries. They're onto me and I've found the child.

Fucking wake up! As he gave Seshan a solid slap"

"A good thaumaturg does not imprecate." Said Seshan clamly.

Like fuck they don't!

Seshan knew immediately he was a scientist, and, possibly a thaumaturg. 'Take this.'

He handed Seshan his hat, with the EM suppressor.

This is the Monday hat.

What happens on a Monday? said Seshan

See over there.

Yes.

See that pretty girl.

Yes.

It's hard to explain, yet in the cultural context you live in, that is God.

I've got go, I think they've found me. Ordain that child and let her wear the Monday hat.

On a Monday?

Of course.

Seshan turned his coat inside out, the inner lining being a vivrant check, donned the hood on his hoodie and bolted out the door. No-one meditating played the blindest notice.

ACKNOWLEDGMENTS

I would like to dedicate this book to my Father, Geoffrey Thomas Baker, we know why.I would also like to thank P.W. for noticing the freedom of the Humming Bird.

Last, but certainly not least, I would like to thank Mrs Jenifer Thorp for inspiring my Love of talking. The English department is the social hub of every good British secondary school, in my humble opinion.

Lightning Source UK Ltd.
Milton Keynes UK
UKHW012244210919
350201UK00001B/2/P

9 781728 393537